Tomorrow's Fortune

Emma Campion, thirty, married, discontented, is a passenger on a northbound train. Her destination: the sea-side and Patrick. So very simple—to deceive one's husband by enlisting the help of one's life-long friend. Or so it seems: 'Dear Geraldine, would you be an angel and invite me to stay with you? David won't think there's anything odd about it.' Geraldine, the loyal friend, complies, and David, the unsuspecting husband, will never be any the wiser. She has covered her tracks, sacrificed to the goddess of retribution, nothing can go wrong. Coincidences, twists of fate—they only happen to other people. But Emma, escaping for three days from the monotony of her daily life to the precarious delights of a lovers' meeting, is unaware of the forces that are combining to effect a shattering upheaval in her circumstances.

And Geraldine, the provider of the alibi, at home in her Warwickshire cottage with her ordered life, her dog, and her disapproval just tinged with envy, finds that she too is caught up in the dramatic consequences that follow upon the news of a sudden and unforeseen catastrophe.

Tomorrow's Fortune

KATHLEEN CONLON

Collins
St James's Place, London
1971

William Collins Sons & Co. Ltd.
London · Glasgow · Sydney · Auckland
Toronto · Johannesburg

First published 1971

© Kathleen Conlon

ISBN 0 00 221839 9

Set in Intertype Baskerville
Made and Printed in Great Britain
William Collins Sons & Co. Ltd. Glasgow

Tuesday

The train burst through a tunnel then hiccoughed, shuddered and jerked to one of those inexplicable railway halts that have the effect of crystallizing the silence inside a carriage to such a painful intensity that its occupants stop talking or coughing or, if they happen to be reading a newspaper, do so with an exaggerated care that may even entail re-reading the same article over again in order not to rustle a page.

Emma Campion, who had once endured a twenty-minute delay somewhere outside Salford in the company of a man with boils on his neck who'd asked her if she'd like to see *Only Two Can Play* the moment they reached Manchester, looked determinedly through the window at a landscape drawn from the muted end of the palette and at a sky the colour of curdled milk. It was a dank February afternoon. Irregular patches of soiled snow lay upon the ground beyond a field full of some hopeless shrivelled vegetable. Beside a run-down farmhouse, a shirt hung, shroud-stiff, from a clothes-line.

But Emma was on the way to meet her lover and, for her, the bleak scene held a poignancy more usually associated with autumn when the view from the window is a sad little English water-colour, as executed by a maiden lady with the beginnings of goitre.

I am on the way to meet my lover, she said to herself at

frequent intervals. The phrase not only evoked former delights but, more important, with its implication of unassailable *rightness*, seemed to justify the tangle of deceit she'd had to weave in order to grasp the opportunity.

In just thirty minutes, D.V., she thought, as the train moved off, I'll look across some room and see him and then chemistry will take over—I'll know that nothing on earth could have prevented me from meeting him. But until that moment arrives, I'm just Emma, sitting on a greasy striped seat, shivering with apprehension, praying to all the gods, in case they exist, that nothing will go wrong, and forcing myself to think ahead to Friday morning (though it doesn't seem possible), when I'll be on this same train facing the other way; same train, same striped seat, same crushed packet of Players on the floor, but travelling back, to greyness, to David, to home.

The thought unnerved her. Hoping for distraction, she picked up a discarded magazine from the next seat and, anxious for omens, looked for her horoscope. Fortunately the magazine was a week old because it was a very dispiriting horoscope.

Aware suddenly of someone's eyes upon her, she looked up. Perhaps she'd been mouthing her thoughts. Still, they said you needn't worry until you started voicing them. On the way to meet her lover. Conveyed not by Pullman with head-rest and taped music, but by a squalid, smelly electric of the sort that seems to be provided almost exclusively for the use of railwaymen coming on and off shift, all donkey jackets and canvas lunch bags and tin tea-cans. The barge she sat in, like a burnish'd throne—but then he was no Antony to sacrifice his all for the sake of a glance from her cornflower-blue eyes. She amended that to cornflower-blue, bloodshot, after a look in her compact mirror. Even the mild vice of four books a week from the library, to fill in the endless days, can leave its ravages.

Into that same compact mirror she couldn't help smiling a smile that contained acknowledgment of her skill as well as some astonishment at the success of her deviousness. Astonishment because it had turned out to be so simple. All it had needed was a letter to Geraldine which elicited the accustomed prompt reply; there'd been a formal invitation to be shown to David and a personal note for herself, affirming the conspiracy. As always, he'd objected just for the sake of objecting, but that wore off. 'Only three days,' she'd said. 'I haven't seen Gerry for ages. No, you can't ring me. She's still waiting for the phone to be installed. I'll ring you. We'll probably go out for a meal one evening and I'll ring you then.' Thank God it had coincided with Gerry's half-term. Seemed more plausible. And what of Geraldine? Faintly amused, disapproving, showed her disapproval more by aiding and abetting than if she'd refused. Had always, right from school, regarded Emma as childish, silly and wayward and undoubtedly considered that David was treated shamefully. But then Geraldine wasn't married to David. Geraldine wasn't married to anyone. Just lived in Warwickshire with a dog called Pinkerton, two herbaceous borders and a stock of alibis.

Emma looked out of the window again. Only one more station and then she'd be able to dismiss David and her shameful treatment of him. Not that it *was* really shameful anyway, or she wouldn't be in such a turmoil, trying to think back and ascertain that she'd provided for any contingency that might arise, enlighten him and cause him pain. And surely, after all this time in the wilderness, all the nights when she reached out and days when she planned, she deserved in some measure the man she was going to meet?

7

She closed her eyes and, for a too-brief moment, she saw the face of the man she was going to meet : the eyelids that drooped at the outer corners, endowing eyes that otherwise would have been too hard and alert with a certain sleepy sensuality which contrasted sharply with the curved severity of his profile. Privileged to be acquainted with the surprising sweetness contained behind the stern cheekbone, the angled nose that would have been a sculptor's delight, she suspected that the unenlightened might form a very different opinion of him, might be deterred—by a disconcerting shrewdness in the face he showed to the world—from seeking further intimacy.

The thought was a comfort to her. It seemed to make him more hers. Though in bleak moments she was fully aware that she did not pervade his life to the same extent that he pervaded hers. But then, you couldn't ask too much, could you? You had to be grateful for even crumbs of undeserved delight. Besides, when she was with him, none of it mattered. David, her husband, would say 'What shall we do? Where shall we go?' He, her lover, told her what they were doing, where they were going. Maybe she'd known prettier, wittier men, but none of those men could ever animate her as he did. To be with him was to be directed, diverted, to be real.

The man nearest the door lifted down his briefcase from the rack and pulled on his gloves. There's *always* a man who knows when you're almost there and on which side the platform's going to be. So soon, Emma thought, remembering a snatch of conversation from their previous encounter : 'What things do you like, Emma?' 'Journeys particularly, limbo in motion, that feeling of being suspended in time.' She also remembered the corollary : 'What things don't you like?' And she'd answered, 'Situations that don't allow me to procrastinate.'

8

And this was one of those situations. Heart racing, she brushed imaginary specks of ash from her coat, checked twice for her ticket. Always the same panic, arrival angst : is it the right station, time, day? Do I look odd? As odd as I look reflected in this grimy mirror? Will he be there? What will I do if he isn't? Please God grant that he hasn't gone under the wheels of a double-decker bus. After all, somebody, somewhere, must go under the wheels of a double-decker bus every day. Too late anyway. We're here. Disassociate yourself. Pretend you're in a play. It's all make-believe. If it's all make-believe, it doesn't matter.

Somehow she was aware of him, standing at the barrier, a split second before she actually saw him. Then he was rushing towards her as though she were the sole survivor of a rail disaster and she was in the haven of two grey tweed arms, putting her suitcase down on his toe as he bent to kiss her, and the ogres of two minutes past were retreating, foiled of their prey.

'I thought it would be a nice surprise to meet you at the station. I got through sooner than I thought I would.'

'You've seen *Brief Encounter* too many times.'

They walked out of the station, down the street to where the car was parked, hand in hand, but not quite in step—yet. Emma made short, brittle comments, afraid to look at his eyes looking at her, afraid to see a trace of disappointment in them. They always needed time to adjust to the rhythm and weight of each other.

'Was everything all right? No snags?'

'No, no snags. And you?'

'Fine. Except that I feel like Mildred Cable having crossed the Gobi Desert.'

It was the nearest they had ever come in half a dozen such meetings to communicating anything of the guile and apprehension that attended their plans. But he suffered

9

from the horrors too. 'I drove so carefully. Everything passed me on the road. Then your train was late. After ten minutes I was having fits.'

She could laugh now at the offerings they made on the altar of Nemesis. Of course they'd meet. People met daily without wondering if one or the other had been overtaken by catastrophe on the way.

In the car she lit cigarettes for them, hoping he wouldn't notice the way her hands trembled, she, who removed splinters from her husband's fingers and threaded fine needles to sew on his shirt buttons without a tremor. She looked sideways at him as he thumbed through the A.A. book, talking of A roads and B roads, and found it impossible to believe in the existence of the woman who had closed the door behind him that morning. How *could* it be possible that someone else should have a claim?

'You think too much.' He'd replaced the road map and sat looking at her, aware of all the misgivings that were chasing each other round her head. 'Emma.'

Cautiously she raised her eyes from contemplation of his tie-pin. By the time they'd reached the level of his lower lip —full, touchingly boyish lower lip—all those misgivings had evaporated.

'Patrick?' The indescribable joy of saying his name to his face.

They kissed, shyly, respecting each other's temporary isolation, but in doing so, the cord of restraint snapped and within minutes she was telling him he still had the nose of a satyr, marvelling that his features had once again assembled into those of the loved one.

Along motorways and side roads they drove, through the pink brick and plate glass of a housing estate, past renovated cottages they yearned to possess, in which they imagined a new, different mode of living, by the side of a turgid canal, once through a farmyard and a scattering of hens. She neither knew nor cared where they were going. She knew only that for three days she would be encapsulated in euphoria between the dreariness that went before and the dreariness to come.

Wednesday

At nine o'clock on Wednesday morning, Geraldine Reid
opened the front door of her Warwickshire cottage and
swore at the birds. Then she picked up the three-quarters-
full milk bottle with the neat hole pecked in its silver top
and swore at the milkman. Having no porch and realizing
this hazard after the first few days of residence, she'd manufactured a bird-proof box for the milk, but every now and
then the milkman succumbed to a bout of idiocy and
ignored it. A case for a strong note tomorrow. She wasn't
going to get up at the crack of bloody dawn during half-
term.

In her tartan slippers, the milk bottle clasped against her
chest, she surveyed the day: black trees, grey silence, except for the rooks in the barn, smoke from the farm across
the fields barely discernible against the sky, the gables of
the mental hospital at the end of the lane still white with
frost. She professed to be unafraid, but was sometimes, in
the night, when Pinkerton's hackles rose and, from beside
her bed, he bayed at an invisible moon. She remembered
Emma's first visit when, glasses of sherry on the fireplace
tiles, they'd talked into the night and Emma had said 'How
can you *live* out here? I'd be petrified.' And then, with her
childish fascination for the macabre, begun to relate tales of
axe murderers, disconsolate spirits, men who entered
through skylights, until they were both too frightened to go

12

to bed. But when Geraldine, alert to every alien sound, had crept into Emma's room for reassurance, she'd found the culprit in deep, untroubled repose, one arm fearlessly exposed outside the coverlet.

At nine a.m., however, such thoughts fail to disturb the most fearful. Geraldine merely sniffed the air, shivered and shut it out again. Cold, even for February. I bet Emma's not cold. She looked up from her cornflakes to the brass letter-rack where Emma's letter lay : thick black italics, sweeping down strokes and erratic punctuation. No, I'll *bet* Emma's not cold this morning. Wonder what he's like, this man? Emma was always catholic in her tastes. Somewhere, up in the box room, was a bundle of letters, among them letters from Emma, posted throughout art school, rep and marriage, some written on yellow paper and pushed into blue envelopes (doubtless the art school period that), others unstamped ('Why is it I can never remember whether or not I've stamped a letter the minute after I post it?'), most of them undated and a great many of them eulogizing some man, John, or David, or once even, Leo, whom Geraldine had met and was convinced had been christened Fred.

She carried her breakfast pots into the kitchen and opened a tin of dog food while Pinkerton wagged a tired tail and shed his moulting hairs all over the place. Pinkerton! Even that had been Emma's doing. 'You need a man about the house,' she'd said. So she saw me as Butterfly? Perhaps I was once. She, or Mariana. Well, now I've found my moated grange and the marish mosses can creep away as fast as they like and I don't much give a damn.

First, to dress, then to shop and then to lunch. An organized day gives meaning to life. Or does it? In her bedroom she looked into the mirror where Emma had posed and said, 'Mirror mirror on the wall, why do you refuse to flatter me?' All the time dimpling and turning her profile from side to side. Vain little creature. Always had been. Geraldine remembered Emma's home, every mirror covered with a cloth because otherwise they couldn't get her to budge, and Emma's father, putting an arm round his daughter's shoulders, saying 'Handsome is as handsome does,' but too obviously proud of her inherited beauty to mean a word of it.

The mirror, which had been so kind to Emma, was merely truthful to Geraldine. Early on, authoritative aunts of the being-cruel-to-be-kind school had said, 'You should always wear tailored clothes, Geraldine. No frills for *you*.'

But she hadn't turned out too badly. A not unpleasing image. Not pretty, not remotely pretty, then neither was Lady Hamilton, nor Nell Gwynn, nor many other successful ladies, if we are to believe their portrayers. They had compensating talents though. She turned from the mirror and began to rearrange the bottles on the dressing table into rigid lines : symmetry, one of her spinsterish obsessions, one of the things that irritated her fourteen-year-olds and caused them to imitate her when she was almost, but not quite, out of hearing. Thank God she was free of them for two days. From the realism of her thirty-one winters, she remembered her original crusading spirit with a mixture of affection and awe.

'Pinkerton!' She called him from a sensual dream on the fireside rug into the kitchen. He sidled, rheumy brown eyes full of pleading. Children and dogs! They love you for what they can get out of you. Emma's like that, all take, leech-like, wilfully ignoring the laws of the nitrogen cycle, that what's taken out must be replaced.

She tidied round in a cursory way. Not that there was much tidying to be done. One misplaced dirty cup or brimming ashtray sent her scurrying to the sink. 'Her administrative qualities are excellent,' they'd written on her last school report. 'Oh don't be so finicky Geraldine,' her mother had said. 'You'll be different when you're married with a couple of kids under your feet.' But two years ago, Geraldine's mother had sat straight up in bed, fallen back again, and died, never to see her prophecy fulfilled.

Outside, though she was muffled to the eyeballs, the cold struck her with a pain like a knife in the lungs. Bound to snow again, she thought, sliding round to the old stable that served as a garage and making a mental note to stock up in case she might be marooned. The car, small and sleek and well-tended, started without protest. She negotiated the rutted lane and lit her first cigarette of the day and remembered her mother.

Snow was dripping from the hedgerows in a dirty trickle. It had been January when her mother died, but similar weather. Standing in the Garden of Remembrance with a drop on the end of her nose and her feet turning to stone, while the vicar swung an urn emitting a thin, obscene stream of what looked like talcum powder to and fro, Geraldine, though numbed with grief, felt curiously liberated. The aunts, black-veiled and crow-like, had clustered round, merging into each other, then and afterwards, clicking their dentures and consoling : 'All alone in the world now.' But she, at the end of the table as befitted her superior mourning position, knew that now there was no one to whom she needed to justify herself.

In town she bought groceries, new-baked bread and also a *New Statesman* to remind herself that out there was a big wide world. Edna Millington was, of course, late. In the Priory Tea Rooms, Geraldine drew pictures in the ashtray with a spent match and chatted to the girl serving her whose mother owned the place and who was Linda Raynor who'd left 4C last summer.

'It's not bad. It's better than school.'

She had smooth straight hair the colour of butterscotch and a body designed for producing babies. Fifteen? Sixteen? In a year or two her life would be nappies and the telly and down the drain would go yet another ten years' state education. Geraldine thought wistfully of university lectureships and students who were there because they wanted to be there.

'You waiting for Miss Millington? I saw her pass about ten minutes ago. Probably gone for dog meat.'

The girl smiled and moved off to the kitchen. Most likely thinking 'A couple of old maids together.' No longer monsters of authority to be feared. Just a pair of pathetic old never-had-its. She'd be wrong though.

But not about Edna, who entered preceded by her voice. 'Heel, Bruno. Just been for his lights. Heel! Thought we'd go to the Bell. Usually not bad on Wednesdays.'

Edna was head of the history department but, had she followed her natural inclinations, would have been a raging success on the parade ground. Geraldine had long ago run out of excuses for refusing Edna's luncheon invitations. Invariably they discussed school. Edna's sole topic was school. They ate shepherd's pie and sultana sponge with custard. That was like school too, but dearer. Geraldine gazed, hypnotized, at the Greek key design which ran from Edna's chin, down her jacket and around her waist and felt Edna's voice washing over her like the waters of Lethe. Necessity makes strange bedfellows. She remembered a staff sherry party during which Emma, on a visit, had excused both of them after the first sherry and collapsed against the wall outside saying 'God! Aren't they priceless! And now where can we get a real drink amongst real people?'

She drove home, thinking of Emma, but more particularly of Emma's husband, that tall, fair, much-abused man whom she liked but could not help regarding with a measure of exasperation because of his continually seeming to take the line of least resistance. For not only did Emma mock him in his absence, but sometimes mocked him to his face and in the presence of others. Such a gentle man, she thought, absolutely type-cast for sacrifice. And so foolish to allow himself to be the target for Emma's malicious tongue.

She thought about him most of the way home. Consequently, she was not, initially, as surprised as she might have been, when she saw Emma's husband's car parked outside the cottage, with Emma's husband inside it, looking pinched and grim and as though he might have been there for hours.

David Campion was twenty-five, engaged to be married to a girl who had her head screwed on the right way, as his mother put it (and that expression, on his mother's lips, was high commendation), and just ripe for a girl like Emma, when Emma came on the scene.

David was doing all right. Everybody said so. His mother never stopped saying so. From the time he was in nappies, she'd determined that he was going to do all right for himself and, if the greater part of his life seemed to have consisted of homework and exams and exhortations to get on, he'd never complained—he knew what was best for him. And it had paid off, you couldn't deny it. He had a good job with excellent prospects and a nice girl who was as determined as his mother that he was going to continue to do all right for himself. David accepted the order of things; it was only infrequently he felt that there were more things in life than he seemed to be experiencing. Not often. But there were times.

Times when Matt, hoisting himself on to the edge of David's desk (that was one of the more irritating things about Matt, he would sit on anything—desks, radiators, even the floor, in preference to a chair), said 'Come out tonight. You're not married yet. Ever heard of wild oats? You're supposed to be getting them sown now, you know, before it's too late. I know for a fact,' Matt adopted his intense, confidential tone, 'that this party will be full to bursting with gorgeous birds just begging for it. Mate, I'm doing you a big favour. I'll bet the estimable Janet doesn't exactly hand it out on a silver platter, does she?'

David winced. Matthew had joined the firm a month ago. Irish, blue-eyed and voluble, it was reputed that he'd been through the typists like a dose of salts; even old Miss Stevenson's heart was seen to flutter beneath her pastel *crêpe de chine* blouse when he put his head round the door. Since his arrival, he'd treated David with the sort of sympathy you'd accord to a sacrificial victim. He must enjoy his last months of liberty. Did he never think of all the female differences he was losing the chance to sample?

'I'll meet you in the Eagle,' Matt said. 'And we'll go on after the pub shuts.'

'I've a hell of a lot of work. And I promised Janet I'd look through some furniture catalogues before she gets back.'

'Jesus! Furniture catalogues. Were you born middle-aged, or what?'

So, at nine o'clock that evening, David was putting on his best suit and selecting one of his less restrained ties, all the while thinking that he'd much rather stay beside the warm fireside and weigh the merits of teak against those of light oak.

'Whose party is it anyway?'

They were in the lift, travelling up to the third floor in a block of luxury flats. You never knew where you were with Matt; one evening it would be bottles of brown in some sordid cellar, the next, cocktails in a Louis Quinze drawing-room.

'Dick and Betty's. Or is it Betsy? Some wildly inappropriate prissy name anyway. Wait till you see her. Big, slate-blue nymphomaniac eyes. No wonder, poor bitch. He doesn't look as though he's got one in him.'

David was never to make the acquaintance of the unfortunate host; the hostess, he gathered, was the one with silver eye-shadow and a chiffon scarf which trailed to the ground and threatened to perpetrate an Isadora Duncan mischief upon her with the first inadvertent footstep. And in such subdued lighting it was easy to step inadvertently. David tripped over an outstretched leg, turned to apologize and spilled drink down someone's back. Luckily that someone was engaged in high-pitched conversation and failed to notice. Matthew was, of course, already holding court to two glossy girls.

Whoever had concocted the punch had either worked from an esoteric recipe, or substituted wildly from a depleted drinks cabinet; David sniffed and tasted and identified the two most pungent aromas as being *crème de menthe* and backache liniment. He searched vainly for a plain, wholesome bottle of beer—the choice seemed to lie between raw spirit and a bottle of something Italian with a foreign body growing inside it. On the whole, he thought he preferred Matthew's cellar parties. At least the booze was unpretentious.

All around him were groups determinedly out-shouting each other; the men leaning back on their heels, the women like brittle Christmas-tree baubles, tinselled and insubstantial, they'd crack if you touched them. They stood, at ease, glasses poised in manicured hands, but their eyes were snakes' tongues, darting, assessing, wondering if any chances were being missed at the other side of the room. No one spoke to him, or made any move to draw him into a circle. This was the sort of party where you needed to be equipped with full egotistical armour. Superficial, Janet would have called these people, phoney, and gone for her coat. Not that she'd have come in the first place.

Matthew, making a sortie to the bar, tapped his shoulder. 'Navel contemplating is better done in private. Come and meet people. That's Prue over there. She's an Honourable. But I'm hoping she doesn't take it too literally. Emma!' He put the three glasses he'd been juggling with back on the bar and pushed through a barrier of humanity to the door. David followed his progress. He saw a bearded man who looked like Svengali and a slight, black-haired girl in a blue frock.

'David, these are Emma and Bernard, or Emma and Bernard, this is David, whichever way round you prefer it.'

Emma smiled, David smiled, Bernard ladled punch and said, 'I wish Betsy could suppress her Lucrezia Borgia instincts when she's making these sort of concoctions. Emma?'

Emma shuddered. 'Not unless there's absolutely no alternative. Whisky please.'

Matthew darted for the bottle. 'How goes *la vie* theatrical Emma? And why haven't I set eyes on you for so long?'

'We haven't been going to the same places.'

She was the first girl David had met who seemed impervious to Matt's charm. It was a refreshing sight to see.

Svengali, who had been smoothing his beard and saying nothing, suddenly hailed somebody and jerked into life—'I have to see Toby'—and shot over to the other side of the room.

'I thought you were supposed to be getting me a drink.' The Honourable Prue, sharp little aristocratic face pinched in peeve, looked from Matthew to Emma and back again.

'Of course darling.' Matt picked up the glass.

'Well I don't want it. I want to dance instead. That is, if you can *bear* to tear yourself away.'

'If you can beah to teah yourself aweah,' Emma said. 'She has the kind of seat designed for a shooting stick. I would even go so far as to say, saddled and bridled, you could enter her for the Derby without anybody noticing anything amiss.'

David looked down at her. There was no malice in her amused features. No need to be with a face like that.

'I've never seen you before,' she said. 'Are you a friend of Matt's? You don't look as though you'd be a friend of Matt's.'

'I'm a colleague of Matt's.' He hesitated to say more in case she was particularly smitten with Matt, or something.

'God's gift to deprived womanhood,' she said. 'He'll be pinching bottoms in a few years, but somehow you can't help admiring his gall.'

'Would you like to dance?' He dreaded an answer in the affirmative. Such daintiness could only serve to accentuate his lumbering inadequacy.

'Not really. My legs are buckling and I'm starving too. Let's go into the kitchen and raid their fridge. Or are you too upright to be involved in such baseness? They'd do exactly the same themselves, you know.'

Suppressing his natural disinclination to presume upon other people's hospitality, he followed her into the kitchen, where she helped herself to a glass of milk and a chicken leg.

'Don't look so disapproving. I haven't had anything since a sandwich at lunchtime. I was sure they could hear my stomach rumbling in the back row of the circle.'

'You're an actress?'

She pulled a face. 'You say it in just the same way as my father does: "My daughter is in Birmingham playing at being Mrs Patrick Campbell. Before that, she spent three

21

years in London playing at being Leonardo da Vinci. Given time, she'll work it all out of her system".'

'And will you?'

'Oh yes, I expect so. Sooner or later you've got to recognize your own mediocrity.' She started on the other chicken leg. 'Have some?'

He shook his head. 'Won't your friend be wondering where you are?'

'My friend? Oh, *Bernard*. I shouldn't think so. Bernard has other fish to fry.'

'Oh?'

'Heavens,' she said, 'can't you *tell*? Bernard is like a sister to me.'

'Then why—?'

'Why do I go around with him? Why not? He's fun. And it's so relaxing not to have to be on one's guard all the time.'

He supposed a girl with her looks *would* have to be on her guard a good deal. Particularly with the Matts of this world. What a waste though.

She kicked off her shoes and stretched her arms above her head. 'Glorious Sunday tomorrow. Long, long sleep.'

'Sunday's your only rest day?'

'Yes.'

'How do you spend it?'

'Doing nothing deliciously. While people like you are in church.'

'People like me?'

'Eminently respectable people. Let me see.' She looked at him with narrowed eyes. 'I bet you're an accountant.'

He was flabbergasted. 'How ever did you know?'

'I'm a witch.'

He could believe it. Three hundred years ago, she'd have been burned at the stake for having eyes like that.

'Twit!' She took a gulp of milk, licked froth from her upper lip and grinned at him. 'I know that's what Matt does, so it didn't take any particular psychic ability to work out that you'd do the same thing. Anyhow, I wouldn't have thought you were one of our lot.'

'Tomorrow,' he said. 'Your day off. Would you come out with me?'

It was out. He hadn't intended to say it. What about Janet? She'd refuse anyway. He must be mad.

'What?'

'The country. We could go into the country. By the river. There's a pub.' Stumbling over the words, the dreaded childhood stammer threatening to return any second.

'Well, I've heard of lightning propositions, but—'

'I'm sorry.'

'Don't be sorry. You don't *look* the fast proposition type at all. Actually there's nothing I'd like better than a day in the country. Except perhaps two days in the country.'

When momentary madness cools, it leaves one with a cold, threatening excitement in the pit of the stomach. He wasn't in her league, he knew it. She belonged to the smooth small-talkers. Really there was no need to worry about Janet, because he was certain that one day of his company would be more than sufficient for this girl.

Emma, whose waking process was normally a lengthy one, woke abruptly, saw first a telephone and a Gideon Bible, thought 'Where am I?' Then an arm sprinkled with curly black hair and thought 'Who am I with?' As soon as her consciousness had adapted itself to answering both these questions: 'You are in a room of a hotel called the Majestic with a man called Patrick Derbyshire and you both have a temporary, mythical London address,' she began to drift back into a comfortable state of semi-wakefulness, but some telepathic signal had roused him too and, kissing her shoulder, he reassuringly said her name.

'What time is it?'

He yawned and, with a mammoth effort, stretched out an arm for his watch. Delicious not to have to keep an eye on it, sometimes a necessity in these situations. '9.27.'

'And what time did we come to bed?'

'Oh, 'bout nine.'

'That's over twelve hours.'

'Emma, is there no end to your talents?' he said, adopting the playful tone that he knew sometimes appealed to her, but abandoning it as soon as he saw it was not camaraderie but reassurance that she required.

So he turned her to him, shaping her body with his hands. She was smooth and warm and responsive. This was the best time; yesterday had been taut, hurried, pent-up passion making their love rapid and almost wordless, it had been necessary for their bodies to remind them, urgently, of the reasons for their meeting; yesterday's fraught excesses had made possible this morning's slow sensuality.

Last night, breaking their tacit understanding that they'd avoid the word, she'd said 'I love you,' as perhaps she had to say 'I love you' to any man she slept with, if only to justify her sleeping with him. And, in that post-coital unguardedness, he'd said, for the first time, that it was good because he loved her too, wondering whether perhaps it was crueller to say it than to refrain from saying it.

He was a man reasonably familiar with the dissimulation necessary in an affair, but Emma was different from any other woman he'd been involved with. Her passivity, her unquestioning acceptance of the limitations of their association, had come as a pleasant but puzzling surprise to him. There'd never been a woman before who hadn't, at some stage, fixed her pensive face and said, 'Yes, but what's going to *happen*?' or words to that effect. It was as if *she* had bowed to some unalterable destiny, as if she had six months to live and realized the futility of vows and plans: the beginning had been unpremeditated, therefore it would be presumptuous to forecast the outcome.

Touching the hair that covered his chest like moss, while he kissed her, she thought perhaps she loved him best when he was behaving instinctively and truest to his natural male self. Endearments could be lies; watching his face, earnest with desire, she was humbled. What was so special about the taste and feel of her particular combination of skin, flesh and muscle that it should arouse him so? At least physical desire could not be faked.

Somewhere a bell tolled, as they lay, hearts drumming against each other, recalling them to consciousness, to separateness. He gazed down into her eyes and it was for that long gaze afterwards that she had come to him, in a train, over miles of frozen ground, then he gently cuffed her cheek. 'We might just get tea and toast if the management's kindhearted.'

'They'll just look at our eyes and wink at each other and secretly envy us.'

Undoubtedly a part, however small a part, of the attraction was the charade, the tingle of apprehension whenever they turned a corner or walked into a bar together. And, a little while later, eating hard toast in a corner of the lounge, which had been served by an unwilling waiter, more interested in exploring his acne than wondering why they were so late down, she reflected that the dangers, real and imaginary, served as an added incentive to their meetings.

She had read somewhere that love generated hunger, but found it untrue for both herself and him. Isolated among silent acres of Turkey carpet, they lowered their voices accordingly and crunched cold crusts merely as a justification to pass on decently to the first longed-for cigarette.

Seeing their images reflected from a kindly distance in a mirror at the far end of the room, she compared the reflection with the reality. Ghastly never to know what you look like to your own eyes—the mirror lies—Narcissus was wasting his time. Reflected, he looked more sallow, sharper, the quality of his alertness exaggerated to a bird-like degree. How different they were! As the mirror had heightened his hard edges, so it blurred her own outlines. And the difference lay deeper than appearance; she would be willing to sit all morning, smoking cigarette after cigarette, demanding nothing more than the occasional mingling of fingers to establish that the current of desire was still flowing, but he was the kind of man who stubbed out his cigarette and stood up all in one action: 'Where are we going to next?' And always she was drawn along, passive in the wake of his vitality.

That vitality had been her one abiding impression of their first meeting. She had no recollection of the way he looked, in fact at each subsequent encounter she was newly surprised by his appearance, always having imagined him, in her fantasies when they were apart, as taller or shorter, slighter or more heavily built. Afterwards, comparing their respective first impressions, he'd told her that what had struck him most vividly was the air she had of being in command of herself—she'd disillusioned him, it was merely her lassitude, her poker face, that misled people. Someone else had introduced them. He'd smiled, shaken her hand, and had been terribly sorry but he absolutely had to dash. She'd been left with nothing more than a blur of blue suit, good teeth and energy, while the someone who'd introduced them said, 'Patrick Derbyshire's all right, but he does tend to overdo the big business thing just a fraction.'

26

Tomorrow's Fortune

It was only the second time they met—the terrible cock-
tail party where she'd stood in a corner, deliberately drinking slowly in case the waitress failed to circulate in her
direction again and listening to everyone else upstaging each
other—that something had begun to generate between them.
She had reached the point when she was wondering if leaving in a surreptitious manner would be less humiliating than
sticking it out stranded when, from somewhere, he appeared
and, facing each other over a plate of rolled-up anonymities
on toast, she'd felt the warm blood pulsing back into her
rigid veins. His conversation was practically a monologue
to which she smiled and yessed and no-ed and was grateful.
Was she dining with anybody? No, she was not. There was
a casserole in the oven and a football match on the television
for David, and in a little, almost pitch-black Italian place,
cracking bread sticks and watching gobbets of wax roll
down the side of the candle-holders, she'd felt the old
familiar, unfamiliar feeling and was quite surprised because
he was not at all the sort of man she'd ever imagined loving.

But even then the decisions had been his, all his. Apparently he had energy and resolve to spare. He had not ques-
tioned her but accepted her passivity as quiescence. Two
weeks later there'd been the flat of a conveniently discreet
and absent friend and a pile of Sinatra records which finally
clicked into silence long after they'd tremblingly discovered
each other in the middle of a big baroque bed that looked as
though it had been acquired from a defunct brothel.

And so he had, by making the decisions, taken the burden
of guilt upon himself. She had not felt the need to admit
that it was anything more than mutual sexual attraction
until the time came when he was ill for a fortnight and
unable to contact her. Then, she knew for sure, screwing up
the sheets during the long, wondering nights, that she had
passed the point when suffering might be avoided.

27

ome on, let's get out of this mausoleum,' he said.
There's nothing, but nothing, quite so depressing as your
four-star hotel between ten and eleven a.m., before the
invasion of musquashed matrons for their morning coffee.'

He went to collect their coats. She tested a flower display
to find out whether the improbably yellow daffodils were
fake and discovered that they were half and half, and
wondered why he hadn't sought out someone with his own
rapid metabolic rate and also wondered, inevitably, about
her predecessors who, for some reason, she saw as yellow-
haired girls with tanned legs and tennis rackets.

'We shall drive and drive,' Patrick said, 'and when we
come upon what they call a beauty spot, we shall stop and
contemplate it and when we are hungry, we'll pull in at the
nearest friendly coaching-inn and partake of their steak pud
and two veg and two glasses of their Tring-bottled bur-
gundy. We'll forget the A.A. book and the map of the district, we'll just go where the car takes us.'

It sounded bliss : driving into the horizon, time and distance, for once, subject to their will, flashing through sub-
urb and idling through countryside, sharing a cigarette and
knowing they could be silent with each other without detri-
ment. She had tried to persuade David to take her for aim-
less drives, but he said what was the point and wasn't there
something Freudian about wanting to be inside a closed
space, forever on the move? Maybe one day she'd do something constructive, learn to drive, surprise him.

Patrick looked sideways at her. In her thick winter coat
at least she looked substantial; sometimes, as she moved, a
slim naked shadow between bedroom and bathroom, he
wondered if she wasn't perhaps just a wraith conjured up
for his own wish-fulfilment. Dear Emma, funny little creature, looking at life child-like, a series of treats interspersed
with grey intervals, inordinately pleased by the smallest sign

of his affection. He wondered about the man David, always picturing him as big and bulky, treading through life in size ten hob-nailed boots, but had never asked. Respecting his reticence, she had not probed for information either, except once when, after love and all barriers down, she'd said, 'What is she like?' And he, stalling, had said, 'Who?' 'No, I shouldn't have asked that question,' she'd said. 'Perhaps it's worse to know than not to know.' So that was where they'd left it. How could he have described Beryl anyway? After twelve years of living with a woman, it was difficult to select the words that could convey anything of the realness of her. Besides, as long as they didn't *make* them real by shaping them with words, they seemed to be less threatening.

Emma kept her hand over his, following its motion as he changed gear. Often, she had the uncanny feeling that in some previous incarnation—back in the primeval slime— they must have known each other. Whatever she discovered about him, the bad as well as the good, seemed to be what, in some shadowy recess of the subconscious, she knew already. Like that other doomed lady had said, 'I am Heathcliff,' so Emma allowed fate to take its course, believing, but not realizing that she believed, that all joy must be paid for in an equal ratio of suffering.

He looked at her, head thrown back, hair spread over the car seat, eyes closed. 'Why are your eyes closed?'

'So that I don't know where I'm going till I get there.'

He grinned and patted her knee. He supposed that something, some day, would have to happen, but dear God, not yet, not for a little while yet.

Patrick kept to his word: they drove, fast and recklessly when the scenery was nothing special, and slowly when they came upon a village or a view which appealed to them.

Only once did they resort to the map and that was after driving down three dead-ends. Eventually Emma opened her eyes to say, 'Oh, how pretty' or 'It's always been my dream to live in a village like this with half a dozen houses and just one pub-cum-general-store-cum-post-office.'

'You wouldn't last a month in the country.'

'Yes, I would. A summer month at any rate. Think of it : fresh eggs and meadowsweet and green all around you.'

'Think of never being able to hop on a bus to see a few fresh faces. You're like me, we're city birds. Our relationship with the countryside is limited to days out and picture-postcards.'

She thought of that grim industrial city in which she had grown up. Not that she'd lived in the grim industrial part of it, but even though you might reside in a Georgian house on Nob Hill, your experience was culled from the city streets and sooty parks just the same. On the way to school, in the bus, you passed through slum areas : children and iron bedsteads and outside lavatories, and the inhabitants were not foreign to you as they would have been to a rural child, even a poor rural child. After all, you met them in those sooty parks and at the fair. They spoke differently and some of them had shorn heads because of lice, but, essentially, though you held your nose when you saw them and they called you stuck-up and tormented you if they had the chance, you had far more in common with them than you had in common with your country cousins who rode to hounds and could tell you all about bulls and cows. It was only as you grew older that the differences between your sort and their sort became ineradicable.

David, her husband, had grown up in one of those streets the bus passed through on the way to school. Not the same city, but it might just as well have been; three steps from the pavement to the front door, lace curtains that were grey again the day after washing, always the end of a meal or the beginning of another one on the table, a front room occupied only on Sundays and Bank Holidays and the claustrophobia of too many people in too little space. She'd expected him to bear life a grudge for having been born, a genetic misfit, into those surroundings, but it seemed that he merely regarded it as everyone's individual duty to escape from them as rapidly as possible. There wasn't much fight in David.

Patrick drove into a lay-by and switched off the engine. It was a lay-by specially provided so that you could look over the wall that rimmed the hill and see a valley spread out before you.

'You're supposed to gaze and gasp at the panorama,' he said. 'I would have thought this sort of landscape was manna to your artistic soul.'

'I find conventionally beautiful landscapes somehow pointless—even boring. What can we see? Fields, divided up by walls, like geometry, a dipping outline of hills that's too perfect—as though they'd been painted on a backcloth, and a few minute, square stone houses, from this distance apparently uninhabited. I like to be in the middle of my beauty. It's the detail: the veins in a pebble, the marks in the sand, even the wallpaper flapping on a half-demolished house. I prefer a row of mill chimneys glimpsed from a train window to this—the mill chimneys are evidence that *people* exist and are carrying on their personal, mysterious lives within them. And it's only because those lives are hidden from your eyes by chimneys and curtains and walls that they are mysterious and fascinating. Once you've penetrated them, they're every bit as boring as your own.'

'Thank you Emma Campion,' he said. 'I will now call upon the next speaker.'

'I think you'd prefer me to be a deaf-mute.'

31

'I think you are a very intelligent, deep-thinking, most beautiful specimen of womanhood,' he said, rubbing his nose against hers. 'And I don't half fancy you.'

That's it, she thought, you fancy me because of my eyes and my lips and various other parts of me. When that fades, what will there be left?

'A cigarette?' He handed her the case. 'And let's go mad and have a swig of brandy.'

He opened the glove compartment: flask, cigarettes, motoring manual. No evidence that anyone but himself occupied the car, no spilled powder or toffee papers or hairdresser's appointment cards. Did he care enough to give it a thorough clearing-out before coming to meet her, or were they just a tidy family?

She drank from the flask and handed it back to him. To drink from the same glass, share the same cigarette—small reassuring intimacies, important pledges between two fastidious people, but perhaps love, after all, was something more than using the same toothbrush.

'Do pointless landscapes always make you look pensive?' he said, flicking ash deftly through the window. There was an expertise about his every small action. It seemed unlikely that in the whole of his life he'd ever spilled or stumbled or been caught off-balance. David, like most big men, was gentle and clumsy, even when loving her.

'Perhaps I'm discovering the secrets of the universe.'

'The only secret of the universe is the knowledge that to survive you have to fight.'

'I shouldn't think you have much patience with the non-combatants,' she said. 'Which is curious, because I'm one of them. Or perhaps it suits you that I am.'

'What *are* you on about?'

'Well, it must be obvious to you by now that I'm the type to let things happen, rather than make them happen. It's always safer to have an affair with somebody like that; they're less likely to kick up fusses.'

'You know,' he said, 'that's just what I thought when I was looking round for somebody to have an affair with. I thought: Emma Campion. She'll do. Doesn't look the type to make a fuss. What were your criteria when deciding?'

There'd always be a woman to love him, even when he least deserved it. He acted upon her like a powerful stimulant, he could make her laugh and she'd come to learn the importance of that.

He screwed the top back on the flask. 'Shall we move on?' He seemed unable to remain in one spot for longer than ten minutes; the doers had always attracted her more than the thinkers.

'Where did *you* do your growing up, Patrick?'

'Wimbledon,' he said. 'Sorry I can't regale you with a more romantic setting, but at the age of six months I came to Wimbledon and stayed there for the next eighteen years until I was sent to Malaya to be made a man of.'

'And did they succeed?'

'Judge for yourself.' He was always reluctant to recount his past history. Once, he'd told her that there were two sorts of people: those who couldn't be prevented from talking about themselves and those who'd talk about anything under the sun, except themselves. The first category was, of course, for the main part made up of women. Most women related everything to themselves. It explained why, on the whole, they were more likely to stay at home and have babies than become cabinet ministers. Anyway, he preferred his women to be women, lovable and aware that they were altogether different from men. His attitude wasn't all that surprising really; look into any history book and you'd find that it was always the men you'd thought of as being the

C

most attractive who were sternly opposed to women's suf-
frage.

They drove on, through a craggy desolation of moorland.
He drove too fast and it worried her. Not at that moment.
She didn't care what happened as long as it happened when
they were together. It worried her in case he drove like that
when they were apart, failing to realize he had a responsibility to her to take care of himself.

'What bliss,' he said. 'To be free of it all for a few days.
Normally, at this time of the day, I'd be wondering if I'd
have the chance to grab a sandwich between appointments.'

'That's what comes of being high-powered.' It was a mistake being drawn to success men; success men just didn't
have the time to devote themselves whole-heartedly to their
love-lives. Much better to find yourself a man with moderate
ambitions. But there were no Patricks among those sort of
men.

'What would you be doing, Emma?'

'That's simple. Having smoked fifteen cigarettes, I'd have
flung down whatever I was attempting to work on in disgust
and gone into the kitchen to open a tin of beans and listen
to some sort of drivel on the radio.'

'I just can't imagine you as an ordinary suburban housewife, making beds and Hoovering carpets and roasting the
Sunday joint.'

'Neither can I. Not even after all these years. I feel as
though it's a temporary role I'm playing and one day I'll get
a different, enthralling offer.'

'How many years?' How little he knew about her.

'Six.'

'Don't tell me you've felt that way for all of six years.'

'No. At first everything was new and sort of—engrossing.
I felt terribly clever and at last grown-up, cooking and
cleaning and making cushion covers. For ages I was in-

volved with the house, getting it just the way I wanted it to be. Finally it was done and, as luck would have it, I met somebody who persuaded me to start drawing again and that kept me going—I ate, slept and lived it for a while. Now it's settled into being just a job. I'm no Van Gogh after all. Then you came along. Perhaps I'm just a woman of brief enthusiasms.' It had been like that in her childhood : riding lessons, tennis lessons, swimming lessons—all to be discarded in their turn, after a season or two; brief enthusiasms could be excused in childhood.

'Perhaps you should have had babies.'

'Perhaps.'

She seemed disinclined to pursue that subject, so he said, 'Just so long as I'm not one of your brief enthusiasms.'

'I'm not sure what the time limit is for brief.' She counted on her fingers. 'Seven months. That's how long you've been an enthusiasm.'

'Is it really?'

He was a man who used every moment of his time, so there was none left to sit and count up how long it was since something had begun. Count on him to remember anniversaries and you'd be sadly disappointed.

'I remember you wore a white frock and you were so tanned I thought you couldn't be English.'

'We'd just come back from Morocco. Very jolly it was. David, of course, had to get dysentery, so I just left him to it and went to lie on beaches. I think that was my second day back. It was raining and I was thinking "England, I love you better from afar and how am I going to readjust to grime and traffic and pallid faces" when I met you. Odd, isn't it? We could so easily not have been introduced. If I hadn't happened to meet Chris and walk along with him, I'd have passed you in the street and thought "What an attractive man" and that would have been that.'

35

'We'd have met anyway. At that party.'

'There were *hundreds* at that party. And if David hadn't been recovering from the dysentery he might have been there too. And if your wife'—she couldn't say Beryl, it would have choked her—'hadn't been in Paris, nothing would have happened.'

'Well, it did. And that's all that matters.' Women. Why did they have to argue everything half to death?

'I went home that night and I couldn't stop smiling. There's nothing so marvellous as that time when you're not quite certain whether or not you're falling in love. If only it could stay that way.'

'You're a great "if only" person, aren't you? I'm saving my "if onlys" for when I'm sixty, by which time I'll have realized they wouldn't have made a scrap of difference.'

Spoke of it as though it would have nothing to do with her, as though, by the time they were sixty, they'd be looking back fondly, and separately, at their foolish optimisms. She touched his sleeve; she was familiar with the feel of the smooth woollen cloth, familiar with the springy curl of his hair, the shape of his mouth and the blind, instinctive softness of his hands, his potency inside her, and yet she could not reach to the centre of him and fuse it with her own centre. As in the dreams, he was always just beyond the reach of her supplicating hands. The dreams that woke her in the middle of the night so she had to reach for David, hold him tight and say, 'You do love me? You won't ever leave me?' Saying it to the wrong person.

'David!' Simultaneously they wound down their windows and for a full minute Geraldine looked into his face, a minute during which she had to convince herself that he was, in fact, flesh and blood, not just a figment of a too-vivid imagination. Perhaps if she blinked, he'd go away.

Oh Emma, *your* administrative qualities were never remarked upon as being excellent.

'Wait a moment until I put the car away.' She drove into the garage, stretching the time it might possibly take to put a car away to its limit. Damn Emma! If she *had* to travel round on leching expeditions, surely she could put some time and thought into ensuring that her alibi wasn't split from top to bottom. Much less humiliating to be the culprit, caught *in flagrante delicto*, than to be the treacherous accomplice. She stood beside the car, fiddling with the handle and jangling the keys, then, realizing that the world wasn't going to come to her rescue by ending at that particular moment, she straightened her shoulders and stepped outside. If only he wasn't such a *nice* man.

He was standing beside the gate, hands pushed down into his pockets, weight distributed evenly on each foot. For a wild moment, she imagined him hearing her confession, then flooring her with a blow from that big fist and turning on his heel. He was the mildest of men, or so Emma said, but worms had been known to turn. She walked briskly past him and up the garden path. 'Let's get inside. You must be frozen. How long have you been waiting?' Play for time. Keep talking. 'When is this weather going to end? How is it in London? By the look of the sky, I'll be digging myself out by tomorrow.'

But, putting the key into the lock, the question came as she knew it must.

'Where's Emma?'

'Pinkerton! Shut up! You remember David. Friends.' Blessed Pinkerton, providing distraction, barking and snarling and battering at the kitchen door. But as soon as she let him out, the snarl became a smile and, with yelps of some unconscious recognition, he was fawning against David's legs.

37

'Take off your coat and sit down. Watch the dog or you'll have hairs all over your trousers. Emma's not here. I'll make us some coffee. I'm sure you must need it. Then I'll explain.'

In the kitchen she poured milk into a pan, lit the gas and broke the virgin foil inside the coffee tin. She thought that if this was Hitchcock, she'd be slipping knock-out drops into the blue-striped mug, then tearing off to tell Emma that all was discovered. That's if I knew where the bloody hell Emma was, she thought viciously, bitterly regretting the phoney invitation. She could hardly deny her own blue disciplined script. In the sophisticated world, there were doubtless ways out of corners like this. For a moment she also bitterly regretted never having penetrated the sophisticated world.

The milk hissed and bubbled at the rim of the pan. She dived across the kitchen and averted the lesser catastrophe. Pouring milk and stirring coffee, carrying it through to the living-room, she was vainly trying to compose the sentence that might soften the impact.

'Thanks, I did need that.' He warmed his hands, huge they were, around the mug. 'Where is she anyway?'

'Sugar? She's not here David.'

'Then where is she?' Expecting to be told that she'd stayed in town shopping, gone to the pictures, back soon. 'I got here about eleven-thirty, hung around for a bit, then went for some lunch. I'd expected her to ring me last night. When she didn't, I assumed you'd stayed in. Though last night would have been too early anyway.'

She didn't understand what he was saying. She took a deep breath. 'I don't know exactly where she is. I daresay that she felt like a few days on her own and I was the only excuse she could think of.'

'You mean she just didn't turn up? Or that she never intended to come here in the first place? What do you mean you don't know *exactly* where she is?' He sat forward on the edge of his chair, requesting the answer she couldn't give him. 'Have you some idea of where she may be?'

'No, she had no intention of coming here and no, I have absolutely no idea of where she's staying. She'll be back on Friday in any case. I think it'll be much better if you wait till then and ask her yourself.'

He caught and held her eyes in his own gaze. It was the first time in her life she'd felt positively shifty.

'I'm afraid Friday may not do. Her father had a stroke in the early hours of this morning. They phoned me at eight, so I contacted the office, then came straight here to collect her and drive up north.'

Coffee was dripping steadily on to Geraldine's lap. Either she didn't notice it or she ignored it.

'He's unconscious. From all accounts, her mother's finally teetered over the brink. It was his sister who rang me. She said that even if we drove up immediately, we might not be in time.'

Emma and Emma's squalidness retreated into the background; Geraldine was ten years old again, a plain, grave little girl, sitting on a tapestry chair, pulling up her long grey socks, while Emma's father showed her his collection of musical boxes and explained their delicate mechanisms: ivory and mother-of-pearl and tortoiseshell, arranged in rows upon the polished surfaces of his study, glinting and lustrous. How he must have shuddered inwardly at her awkward, curious, chubby child's fingers. Robert Sainter, the man who, while Mrs Sainter rested in a shaded bedroom plagued with a mysterious illness called nerves and Emma ran down the garden laughing with malicious glee, had bathed her grazed knees and mopped her face with a big

39

white initialled handkerchief. Robert Sainter, the first idol of her life.

'He won't *die*, will he?'

'I just don't know. You know what hospitals are like. You've a job to find out what's wrong, let alone the chances of living and dying. He's on the danger list.'

The memory of those musical boxes was all that remained from that period of puzzling joy and anguish. There had been one, Victorian, she supposed, with the figure of a dancer, a Columbine, with pink enamelled roses on her skirt. He'd told her the name of the tune. It was 'Traumerei' and it had haunted her. She'd learned to play it on the piano. She remembered that piano with its green pleated silk front and candlesticks and her mother's voice, raised : 'Not that one *again*. Doesn't she teach you anything else?'

'So you see,' David was still there and still menacing, 'it's imperative that I find out just where she's decided to slope off to.'

'If I knew, David, I'd tell you. She didn't drop the slightest hint of where she was going.'

'Or who she was going with? Come on, Geraldine. I may look a fool, but I know and you know that I know she hasn't gone off to commune with nature. Don't you object to being used?'

'It's hardly a question of that. At the time, it seemed unimportant. After all, if this hadn't happened, nobody would be any the wiser. And remember, before you start accusing me of collusion, the discrepancies in your marriage aren't my responsibility.'

There! That was said. She hoped that whoever had averred that attack was the best form of defence had known what he was talking about. But she didn't dare look at his face and instead poked round in the coal-scuttle for non-existent coal.

'Where do you keep it?' He stood up and took the box out of her hands. She'd forgotten that he was the sort of man who walked on the outside of the pavement and carried heavy shopping baskets.

'There.' He'd filled it to the brim. 'That should last you until tomorrow. It can't be very pleasant going out there on a winter's night. Whatever prompted you to bury yourself in the countryside?'

'Mainly it was the chance of a place of my own and the price I could afford rather tended to dictate the situation. There aren't many people who could face a seven-mile drive every time they ran out of cigarettes. But in the summer it's glorious. I see things I'd only ever read about previously.'

They were being deliberately polite, keeping face at all costs. The alternative would have been a scene and neither of them, even though distressed, was sufficiently uninhibited for that. Nevertheless, conscience demanded some sort of an apology from her. What must it feel like to be the cuckolded husband having to face the abettor of the cuckoldry?

'I'm sorry, David. Sorry, that is, that things should have turned out this way. But you know Emma—she doesn't seem to see things like other people.'

'Oh, I know Emma,' he said. 'After six years, I know Emma like I know the Brazilian jungle. I know she's vague and thinks it's a virtue. I know she takes a size ten in dresses and a size five in shoes. I know she smokes twenty cigarettes a day, she likes Mozart and Scarlatti, that she was never destined to be a housewife and has a disgusting habit of stubbing out fag-ends in saucers, but when it comes to knowing what motivates Emma, I haven't a clue. She's like an onion: you peel off one layer and find another and so on and so on, until you're left with nothing.'

'That's the longest speech I've ever heard you utter.'

'That's right. I'm the quiet type. The only asset I have is that I'm successful at my job. I make sufficient money to afford those things which help to ease the difficulties of life. But I'm useless when it comes to high-powered intellectual conversations or injecting excitement into the common round. She's bored to tears with me, you know that? I can see her eyes glaze over as soon as I enter the room. I don't seem able to provide the stimulation she needs. God knows I've tried : holidays—the first day's fine, then you find her sitting silent with a drink, convincing herself that the fun is somewhere else and she's missing it.'

They were sitting with their backs to the window, staring deep into the fire and both occasionally and inadvertently nudging Pinkerton who snarled and shifted his rump. Now Geraldine rose to get her cigarettes and saw that the snow, forecast for days, was at last fulfilling the prediction and falling silent and thick.

'Just look at this. Flakes the size of half-crowns.'

He joined her at the window. Tall herself, he was one of the few men who could make her feel protected. 'It must have been snowing ever since we came in. I bet it's a good inch thick already. I'd better get moving. I expect she'll telephone tonight from wherever she happens to be holed up.'

'And if she doesn't?'

He shrugged. 'Perhaps the police? Messages over the radio and flashed on to cinema screens. I very much doubt whether *The Times* personal column would prove to be fruitful : "E come home. All is forgiven." I suppose she'll have better things to do than read the paper in the mornings. Oh she'll phone. I've no doubt of it. She'll be careful to cover her tracks. Well, Geraldine—' He put on his overcoat. He seemed uncertain whether or not to hold out his hand and finally compromised with an awkward tap on her shoulder. 'Perhaps happier circumstances next time. Thanks for the coffee. Well—'

'Goodbye David.' She cut short his dithering by opening the door and, closing it behind him, leaned back against it, feeling rather like someone who's visited the dentist envisaging wholesale extraction and found that all that was necessary was a small filling.

She lit her cigarette and inhaled deeply. God, what a mess. If it hadn't been tragic, it would have been funny. In a week or so, there'd be a rambling epistle from Emma. Perhaps Emma would find her tin trunk on the doorstep when she got home. Though she couldn't imagine him as the go-and-never-darken-my-doorstep-again type. Anyway, one thing was certain : that was the first and last time she'd enter Emma's conspiracies.

A loud knocking cut sharply into her reverie. Who in the name of God could that be? A proper little Geraldine-is-at-home-to-visitors day it was turning out to be.

His shoulders were covered with snow, and particles of flake clung to his eyelashes. 'Back so soon?' she said. 'Or is it the Yeti?' But he didn't smile.

'Where's your nearest garage?'

'There isn't one until you get into town. Why? Don't say you've broken down.'

'Ten out of ten for perception. That's exactly what's happened. I knew there was something wrong. I meant to take it in today but in the general panic I forgot all about it.'

'Where are you?'

'At the end of the lane, pulled on to the grass verge. I'd have some sort of a go myself, but you can't see your hand in front of your face out there.'

She wanted to say, 'Have you ever had the feeling that

43

it's just not your day?' She stifled the impulse. 'There's a phone box about two miles away. I'll try to get help from there.'

'*I'll* go, if you'll lend me your car. I couldn't possibly let you go out in this.'

'You probably wouldn't find it. Forget the gallantry until the weather improves. I shouldn't think I'm any less capable anyway.'

'I didn't mean that,' he said. 'It's just that I'd be worried.'

'There's no need to worry.' But once outside, she was less confident. The snow had increased to blizzard intensity. Her windscreen wipers were useless against it and for most of the way she drove blind and sweating with fear. Without familiar landmarks, the distance was impossible to gauge and it was partially instinct which guided her to the right place. If you could judge it in comparative terms, she thought, how very much more terrible it must be to die in isolation than to die in company.

She tried three garages—the only three. Their replies were identical. She must be joking madam. It had been snowing since midday throughout most of the county. There were six-foot drifts on nearly all roads except the motorway and accident reports were coming in by the minute. The A.A. were warning motorists they drove at their own risk. Perhaps tomorrow morning after the council had de-rusted their snow ploughs. Why did this bloody country never prepare itself for the inevitable?

So that seems to be that, she thought bleakly, giving the operator the number of the hospital in which Emma's father might even now be breathing his last.

'Are you a relative?'

Geraldine, having just put in the last of the small amount of change they'd mustered between them, cursed bureaucracy and explained.

'There's been some slight improvement, but he's still critically ill.'

She drove home. Not quite so blizzard-like now. It had settled into a steady fluttering that seemed likely to continue throughout the night. Oh God, it was going to be a very jolly evening.

Pinkerton whined at the door for ten minutes after Geraldine had left and then gave it up as a forlorn hope. 'Have you been deserted too, poor fellow?' David said. 'But she'll be back. So will Emma. Trying to conceal the bloom on her face.'

Talking to oneself came quite naturally here. The quiet was uncanny. No next-door neighbours, buses, train whistles, road-workers, not even in the summer. Just the birds and the wind. He wondered if Geraldine talked to herself. She seemed far too well-balanced to indulge in anything like that. He looked around him. It was just the sort of room you'd expect her to live in: stripped wood and tiles and clear expanses of painted wall, relieved only by a Persian rug of brilliant hue and a Chagall print above the fireplace; books, row upon row of them, stacked in alphabetical order, he discovered, and a pile of records, all fitted correctly, edges inward, into their sleeves; elegance, symmetry and a touch of austerity, mirroring the woman herself. His own home, he supposed, was elegant—they'd paid Emma's friend, the interior designer, enough to make sure it must be elegant: purple mosaic tiles in the bathroom and Douanier Rousseaus as you went up the stairs. His own tastes were less exotic, but Emma had been brought up among Chippendale and Spode and restraint, not in a house where, for the first ten years of your life, the bathroom was a tin tub in front of the living-room fire on Friday nights. Emma had found all that very romantic: his thirteen-year-old

45

paper round, his mother doing other people's housework before coming home to do her own, his father laid off work for three years with his back. They'd met during that period when people were falling over themselves to write the definitive novel about the working classes and she was *so* bored with her theatrical friends who pretended they lived in council houses whereas actually Daddy was on the board, or owned the mill, or something. By the time she'd discovered he wasn't really angry about anything, he'd become a habit, the perfect foil to set off her sparkle. For she had sparkled in those days, before the cage closed round her. He hadn't been able to take his eyes off her. She was like no girl he'd had before and he was terrified that she'd drift out of his life as casually as she'd drifted into it.

And she would have done too, had the circumstances been different, he knew that now. Every one of those glittering days of courtship had been a kind of falsehood. Why couldn't people make damn' sure they meant what they were saying before they said it? On the other hand, why did people like himself allow their ears to be so dulled that they believed it?

Geraldine seemed to go very much on Jane Austen. That figured. She'd probably have been wildly successful in the days when mental subtlety and precision counted for a lot. You'd be more likely to find Emma's life-type among the pages of the Brontës: one of those fools-to-themselves women, convinced that all unhappiness was due to circumstances beyond their control. And what book would contain him? *The Diary of a Dupe*, no doubt, if it had ever been written.

'Where are you now, Emma?' he said to the alabaster figurine on the bookshelf, a figurine with wings, unclipped. 'Or, worse than that, what are you doing?' He felt sheer physical jealousy like cramp in the stomach. That was the

46

trouble : you had to dig down so deep, beneath the layers of sexual jealousy and wounded pride and fear of change to find your true feelings. But there were facts, facts like marriage, six years of it. Even if it wasn't as it should be, it *was*. At least the man, if there was definitely a man, would have six years of shared experience to compete with—if any of it mattered to her. Or was he just a man taking what was offered to him for as long as it lasted? For a moment, he felt fierce rage against the unknown man. To think of his Emma like that. His Emma. Anybody's Emma. How could she allow herself to be diminished in that way?

In the bottom left-hand corner of the bookcase was a photograph album. He lifted it out. Normally he wouldn't dream of prying into other people's belongings; lately he'd found himself behaving in a way completely alien to his normal code of ethics. And he found what he'd expected to find : a record of those years he knew of only from hearsay : Emma and Geraldine at ten, holding hands and scowling; Emma and Geraldine perched on a damp and jutting crag at the summit of Helvellyn, all teeth and thighs; school photographs : even at fourteen she stood out in the identical navy-blue ranks. He snapped the book shut. Why couldn't God have made her plain? As if it wasn't bad enough that she should have grown up in that household of gracefully conducted wrong-doing. But to be beautiful as well—it was no wonder she was as she was.

He thought of Robert Sainter, tucked tight and white into a hospital bed. What sort of a bargain with the devil had he made? How civilized Emma made it seem whenever she talked about it : 'My father is attractive to women'; he had not thought it civilized that day Emma took him home and they bumped into her father escorting the latest of his conquests through the door of a restaurant. Not as if it was just one woman. He could have understood that and perhaps sympathized. But how could you sympathize with a man who seemed bent on conducting a comprehensive biological search through the female species?

All of that looked like coming to an end now. What did you think about, if you were capable of thinking, when you were desperately ill? Were you totally concerned with the struggle to stay alive, or did the spectres of your sins and omissions return to haunt you? A clock chimed the hour and he jumped a foot. Geraldine, please be careful, he prayed. I just couldn't stand any more disaster today.

How long had Emma been planning this escape? That it was a deliberate, planned action, rather than an impulse, made it more dreadful. He imagined the weeks of hoping and worrying and checking over minute details that must have preceded her flight. The letter to Geraldine and the waiting each morning for the post, pausing before opening the reply, praying that her scheme would go unopposed. The letter to Geraldine. How long had he been staring at it before it registered? There. In the letter-rack. White envelope. Black ink. Italic nib. Geraldine had not had the opportunity to remove it to a less conspicuous position. Besides, she wouldn't expect him to read her mail. He read it.

So Geraldine had been telling the truth: there was no destination mentioned, just, after the obligatory general preface, 'would you be an angel and invite me to stay with you for three days from Tuesday 3rd? I won't go into details, but it would mean so much to me if you could help. David won't think there's anything odd about you asking me to visit you. I know you'll read this and purse your lips just as you always did when you thought I was behaving recklessly, but really, unless it's possible for me to get away, I don't think I can carry on.'

Stomach cramp again. He replaced the envelope carefully at just the same angle as it had been. At least she hadn't descended to coy, feminine intimacy. She probably realized that approach wouldn't cut much ice with Geraldine. In fact the letter contained no incriminating evidence. The neutral reader would have assumed that the writer wanted nothing more than a few days to be alone. But Geraldine hadn't understood it to mean that. He believed she was a woman who looked straight at you, and she hadn't been able to look straight at him.

His eye followed the convoluted pattern in the rug: scrolls and roses and curlicues, one leading into the other, no ends emerging anywhere. Like his own thought processes, always returning to the same impenetrable muddle. He walked to the window. What was keeping Geraldine? Not a small matter of a snowstorm surely? There were more serious matters than snowstorms and every second counted. If he could be home to wait for her call tonight—after all one night was less binding than three nights. And they might be in time to see her father. She'd be eternally grateful to him for that.

You stupid sod, he thought, you stupid weak-willed sod. Ready to prostrate yourself. She'll trample on you. It's her nature. To her, nothing is worthy of respect unless it's a challenge. God knows how long this liaison has been going on, God knows how many lunchtimes and afternoons on rented beds there have been. Perhaps not even rented beds. Perhaps this man, if there is a man, has no ties and can offer her the hospitality of his own bed. But somehow he felt that if the man existed, he'd be a married man. Emma didn't seem to be interested in anything that came to her without a struggle.

If she was in the position of most wives, financially dependent upon their husbands, she wouldn't have found it as easy to go cavorting across the countryside. But Emma had a good income of her own. And if her father died she'd never have to want for money as long as she lived. He remembered his mother, head in hands, tears spilling through her fingers, saying that if only she could get away, start afresh, life might be different. But she couldn't get away. She didn't have the money. She was tied in poverty to a man for whom she felt only compassion, and by the time he was able to make it possible for her to get away, she could no longer make the effort. Women like Emma, women who had been granted everything, who had no real troubles so set about creating some—they sickened him.

But once it had been different. That first Sunday, they'd walked beside the river, the sun through the leaves dappling her face and her hair. She'd been so gentle and serene, raising her face, her eyes closed, to be kissed. And, kissing her, he'd trembled because, beside the river, among the trees, he'd found all he ever hoped to find and knew that nothing that followed could be as exquisite as that moment. Covering her mouth with his mouth, her eyelids would close and blot out the trace of some past sadness that lingered in her eyes. All his desire had been contained in those kisses; even the act of love when it eventually occurred could not approximate to that first blind reaching-out to draw her close to him. And now it seemed he was her jailer and she was a pinned butterfly able to manifest her dazzling sweetness only when freed to walk along river banks with strangers.

'Come *on* Geraldine.' Pinkerton thrust a moist sympathetic nose at him. Dogs. At least if you fed them they remained faithful. Perhaps Geraldine had made that painful discovery. If Emma did phone tonight, he'd play along with her. Offer to come and pick her up, listen to the terror in her voice as she sought for reasons why he shouldn't do that, agree, and let her travel home on a train all unaware that she was found out. Treachery breeds treachery. He had never consciously allowed her to suffer; it would be a new

experience for him to see what changes, if any, suffering
wrought upon Emma.

'I can remember spending a holiday in this district when
I was very small,' Emma said. 'We rented a cottage and for
three weeks my father didn't shave. My mother threatened
to shoot him with a silver bullet when the moon came up.
That was when I think they still enjoyed being married to
each other.'

'And now they don't?'

'Not for years. She retreated into illness and he met
Flora.'

'Flora? How very exotic.'

'She wasn't at all. She was understanding and kind and
good for him. They were together for five years, until she
died. Well, together apart, if you see what I mean. I liked
her a lot. I could get through to her in a way I couldn't
get through to my mother. We seemed to have a lot in
common with each other. Not surprising really, is it, the
way things have turned out?'

To counteract this sudden flash of bile, he heaped her
plate with apple-meringue. 'So, pre-Flora, it was all smooth
sailing and you were a normal, happy, well-adjusted little
girl?'

'I was *never* those things. And Flora was effect rather
than cause. It seemed that at some point deadly boredom set
in. But there were good times, like the time we came here.
There's something I remember. Pass me the map.'

He did so and watched with affection the bent head, her
eyes so short-sighted that her nose almost touched the map,
her forefinger tracing erratic routes through the terrain. He
summoned the waiter. There weren't many people in the
restaurant they'd chosen for lunch and every word they
uttered seemed to ring back at them and everyone else from

the vaulted, mock-beamed ceiling and Emma, disconcertingly, did not seem to feel the need to lower her voice even when imparting quite intimate bits of information.

'Here!' she said. 'Here, just outside this village. There was a hall set in acres of parkland and a little chapel where we signed our names in the visitors' book. I was eight years old and I think it was, will always be, one of the happiest days in my whole life. Somewhere there was a river—a stream perhaps—the rushes and weeping willow sort. Everything seemed to be green and gold. Midges bit my legs and I cried because I thought they were mosquitoes (I'd been reading an adventure story about Africa and blackwater fever), but he bathed them and told me I'd still have legs like Betty Grable. We ate peaches—I can taste those peaches now—and drank ginger beer from a stone jar. It was one of those days when to be alive seems a gift. We couldn't go and look at it, by any chance?'

'Of course. Why ever not? I'll see if the porter can give me an idea of the route.'

She stayed to finish her coffee. He's humouring me, she thought. Why am I so terrified of boring him? Usually it's the other way round—I'm wary of people in case I find them boring. And why does he never want to know about me in any sense but the physical one, when I could sit and listen for a year if only he'd unburden to me?

In the car park she turned up the pale grey fur of her collar around her chin and looked up at the sky.

'You're dressed to match it.' He followed her eyes. 'I should think there will be more snow before long.'

'That would be marvellous. A couple of phone calls: "Haven't you seen the road conditions on the news?" And we could spend delicious days together quite legitimately.'

He agreed with a smile, knowing that fate could not be so

kind and that perhaps it was as well, perhaps the essence of their relationship lay in its brevity.

It took them an hour to find the right road. The porter he'd asked had raised an uncomprehending eyebrow and passers-by were either new to the district or else gave them complex and inaccurate directions. He was close to abandoning the search when she said, 'I recognize it now. It's like one of those experiences people describe when they actually see a place they've dreamed about, except that of course I've really been here before. You see that farm? That's where we used to get milk and eggs.' And, a little later on, 'Look! The cottage. Oh God. Who ever painted it in those foul colours? It used to be black and white, decidedly mock-Tudor, but charming all the same. What I can't understand is that the distance between the two seems so short. It used to take us a long time to walk there and back in the mornings.'

'Your legs were shorter then,' he said. 'This looks as though it might be your place. Do double iron gates topped with lions rampant mean anything?'

'Yes, this is it. It looks tidier somehow.'

'I don't really see how you expect to recapture some golden summer on a day like this,' he said, turning the car. 'Still, if it satisfies a pet whim, I suppose you must be allowed to indulge it.'

'It's far more than a pet whim. It's—' She closed her mouth. She didn't have the words to explain to him that somehow it was intended to be a gesture of their closeness, that by making her recollections mutual, it would involve him more deeply.

The driveway was bounded with coniferous trees, so it wasn't until they turned the last abrupt angle that stark reality hit her in the face.

'Time they weeded their car park,' he said, pulling on the handbrake.

'No, this isn't the car park,' she said quietly. 'This, as far as I remember, was it.'

'It?' He surveyed a desolation of uneven flagstones and jutting foundations. 'You're sure you haven't made a mistake? Perhaps they were the wrong rampant lions.'

'No. This was it,' she repeated obstinately. And suddenly he glimpsed something of the child in Emma: the inability to come to terms with disappointment or to accept the ravages of time.

'I don't understand how it could have been razed to the ground so utterly,' he said. 'Fire seems unlikely. And they don't usually demolish places of historic interest out of hand. Let's find your chapel, if that still exists. Someone or something in there might be able to throw light on it.'

The chapel did exist. It was probably quite fashionable to be married from : bride and 'groom pictured against ancient carved portals—'What a pretty little place'—a monument to an architect who'd dithered everywhere between Late Gothic and Early Renaissance. 'And we complain about council houses!' Patrick said.

'I remember it as being quite beautiful.'

'I seem to remember thinking glittery Christmas cards and yellow socks were quite beautiful when I was a child.'

She moved away from him. 'Sometimes you mock too much,' she said.

'All right, all right, don't get into a huff. It's just that I prefer you less intense.'

They applied for the key to an inmate of one of the adjoining almshouses and asked if she could give them any information. She stood there, all carpet-slippers and disinterest and no, she couldn't, it was long before her time.

Whispering in the church the way they whispered after

love in the shaded quiet of hotel bedrooms, they looked up in topaz and violet shadow to the lozenge-shaped windows where Christ preached to an absent congregation and was then crucified in an anatomically improbable position. Moving through rows of dusty, spineless Songs of Praise, Patrick recited the message of a plaque : 'Consecrated to the memory of Sir Edmund Upton, 1537.' Then reached a noticeboard : 'The annual Spring Fayre—they've got to be joking. Hey! I've found your visitors' book. It's in Sanskrit though. No it's not. I've deciphered something. 1950. That's the earliest entry. How long is it since you were here?'

'Twenty-two years.' She leaned back against the font, hands in pockets. 'Daft really. The whole idea was daft. Let's go.'

And they would have gone, had their exit not been impeded by a procession of what could only be ladies of the church headed by their vicar.

He beamed. He looked as though his mouth frequently ached with the effort of beaming. 'Ah! The caretaker said she'd already let a couple have the key.' Not only did he beam, he blinked also. 'It's a fine little chapel, isn't it? Some of the finest stained glass of the period. Such a pity it's too far off the beaten track for many people to bother. I told my ladies—we've been to the Cathedral you know—it would be a shame to miss it out when we were in the area.'

He began to marshal his flock and with a sweep of his arm both Emma and Patrick were drawn into their midst and found themselves walking back obediently into the body of the church.

A murmur arose among the ranks of be-hatted ladies. 'Masterly, masterly,' said the one next to them, raising a shining face, and the others nodded fervent agreement. She was clearly their spokeswoman, to be relied upon for the incisive phrase.

'The stained glass, Mrs Grainger? Yes indeed. I'll pass on to that in a moment, but first I want you to look at the screen. Does anyone notice anything in particular?'

A hesitant voice broke the silence. 'It's oak?'

'That's a good observation, but I meant something rather more specific.' He gave them another moment to guess, but could not contain himself longer. 'If you look carefully, you will notice several small holes in the upper part. Bullets! Fired in 1644 when this House was one of the last Royalist strongholds in the country. With three hundred troops the family resisted the Roundhead forces until finally the siege was lifted and Cromwell's troops defeated by Prince Rupert.'

This sounded like a man who, Sunday after Sunday, intoxicated by the sound of his own voice, had them snoring in the pews. It could go on for ever and Patrick had a low boredom threshold.

'I'm sorry to interrupt, but we're in something of a hurry and we wondered if you could tell us about the House.'

Emma looked at his solemn profile: the Roman nose she joked about, the mouth which was just saved from inflexibility by its fullness, shadow of the heavy beard which seemed to encroach upon rather than grow from beneath the taut and tender skin. There was an unconscious severity about his features which prompted people to inquire if he'd just had bad news. Though she realized his reasons for interrupting were not her own reasons—he merely wanted to get the whole business over and done with—it could not diminish an unexpected pang of pure, unmingled love which she felt must be read clear and bold upon her face even by the respectable matrons around her who had probably long since forgotten such things existed.

'Apparently,' the vicar had a tone for imparting facts quite distinct from his sermon tone, 'apparently it was sold

56

to an American about twenty years ago and transported back to be re-erected out there. I expect the family fortunes were at a low ebb and, after all, they do have another seat. A sad little episode though. One would have imagined that there were alternatives.'

They left him, deflected from his subject quite, telling his audience about other ill-fated ancient piles.

'There's always my river,' Emma said. 'Down a sort of lane—'

'Emma. It is five o'clock. I am very cold. Your river will doubtless be frozen over or drained to make way for a fly-over or something.' He put his arm round her and drew her to the car. 'Trying to re-create the past is never a very successful exercise. We're here now and we're together. Let's make the most of it.'

They drove back through the avenue of trees which reminded him of that Dutch painting: Van? No, Hob—Hobbema, that was the fellow. It used to hang in the common room at school. Never *could* stand that painting.

Emma smoked silently and dismally, remembering the delight with which her father had shared his knowledge. This was the house, he said, to which Henry Tudor had brought his Elizabeth, his white rose of York, and he'd coloured in for her a picture of retainers and livery, dogs and falcons, huge feasts and wimpled damsels. Here there'd been bloodshed and treason. When he told her, how different it had seemed from the close print of the textbooks. She thought fondly of that least boring of men, her father.

At length she said, 'I wanted to show you a bit of my childhood. There's nothing I can share with you. We know so little of each other.'

It would have been unkind to tell her that those kind of exchanged recollections could have no place in their relationship, so instead he said, 'Cheer up Emma. I'm going to find an olde English tea shoppe. I have a sudden craving for tea and crumpets, to be eaten among a collection of copper warming pans.'

'Tea-and-crumpet tea shoppes are part of the English myth. We're much more likely to find Formica table-tops and Perspex coffee cups.'

'That's better.' He took her hand. 'When it comes to Emmas, I much prefer the light-hearted version.'

She smiled and allowed herself to be won over. For the rest of the way she acted gay, deliberately suppressing the frightening thought that one day she might not be able to summon up the light-hearted Emma for him at all.

Geraldine shook the snow from her coat and opened the door. He was sitting there just as she'd left him. 'For heaven's sake take off your overcoat,' she said irritably. 'It's pretty obvious that you're not going anywhere tonight.'

'What did they say?'

'What could they say? With luck and a few efficient snow ploughs, it will be picked up in the morning. Oh, and the hospital said—after I'd identified myself as a clean-living, fully paid-up member of society—Mr Sainter has shown a slight improvement.'

He rose and stood at the window, moving from foot to foot in agitation. 'What can I do?'

She flopped down into the place he'd vacated. 'You haven't a wide choice, have you? You *could* get a train home, but by the time you missed connections you'd probably be too late for Emma's call anyway and short of walking you wouldn't get to the station. The roads are impassable. You'll have to stay here until morning.'

'There must be some alternative.'

'Back to the phone box and dial 999 you mean? Look. Emma was going to phone you tonight. Right? When there's no reply, she'll naturally be worried. So she'll try again in the morning, perhaps even phone your office and they'll let her know what's happened. Failing that, she'll be bound to ring again tomorrow night, by which time you'll be home by some means or other. Of course if you *want* to do a Scott of the Antarctic that's entirely up to you, but it seems somehow more reasonable to stay put until tomorrow.'

He considered. 'I suppose you're wondering why I'm bothering about Emma, when it's pretty certain Emma won't be bothering about me.' He took off his coat. 'It does seem the best plan.'

'It's the *only* plan.'

'I'm very grateful to you,' he said. 'I'm not putting you to any trouble—?'

Probably if he'd been crawling across the desert for a week and finally reached an oasis encampment he'd have first asked if he was putting anyone to any trouble before he drank.

'I'll get my bag out of the car then.'

'OK. And I'll see about some dinner. Rustic living teaches you one thing and that's to keep your larder stocked and your cigarette box full.'

She moved round the kitchen in her methodical way, reaching down pans, lifting vegetables from the rack, taking the right sort of knives from the right drawers. She was a little apprehensive about the long evening ahead of them. In different circumstances, of course, she might have welcomed it. He was, she suspected, a man of integrity, but so unassuming as to have left an almost negative impression on her. Not that she'd really seen much of him—perhaps half a dozen meetings in all : the first time at a party in Birmingham when Emma, whose most recent escort had been an unpublished and never-likely-to-be-published poet, had said, 'There's something tremendously sweet and dependable

59

about him,' and then pulled him, unwilling, into the middle of the floor where he had effectively demonstrated that he was one of nature's non-dancers. Then there'd been the wedding which, understandably, had been swift and unshowy : the register office, followed by food and drinks at Emma's home, served by waitresses who wore caps over their foreheads à la Wimbledon Ladies Championships 1925. He hadn't said much then and Geraldine, head held rigid under the unaccustomed hat, had wondered momentarily whether perhaps he had a speech impediment or whether he shone only in more intimate gatherings. The other occasions had been flying visits during which she and Emma had so much to say to each other that his silence went unnoticed. The only thing that had really struck her was his pleasant, straightforward manner and the pity of it that such an apparently vulnerable man should be obsessed with a professional assassin like Emma.

'It won't be long. I'm doing chops. If I begin anything more exotic we'll be eating each other before it's ready.'

'Don't worry about me. I'm used to erratic meals. Emma's a great one for forgetting, so sometimes it's a choice between eating at one a.m. or resorting to eggs. No, that's not strictly true.' He was not the man to hit below the belt, even when faced with his wife's probable adultery. 'Usually it's all right. Just sometimes—'

'Let's see if the rest of the country is battling bravely through snowdrifts,' she said briskly, turning on the television, and they sat watching Scottish snow ploughs, isolated Yorkshire farmhouses and the white plains of Dartmoor, both wondering which particular barrier Emma might be imprisoned behind. They also sat through a regional broadcast which verified the garage proprietors' reports, but even their conversational pauses seemed preferable to the particularly inane quiz game which followed.

'Shall I?'

'Yes, switch it off by all means. I shouldn't think it's quite up to your intellectual mark, is it?'

The remark was quite devoid of malice. She imagined herself as he, with a little help from Emma, must see her: the formidable lady scholar, the career woman. She remembered those female dons with long frocks and woolly hair who had served to increase her determination to escape from the academic cloister into the world where real people battled with real problems, not just the fine translational nuances of medieval French or whatever.

'Nor yours, I would imagine.'

He stretched his incredibly long legs towards the hearth. 'My profession doesn't demand great intellectual powers, just the ability to think logically and precisely.'

If ever there was a man you'd look to for mending fuses or killing spiders or sorting out the problems that lie outside the scope of the average female mind, that man was David. She would have said that he was just the sort of man Emma needed, but then she supposed that the difference between what Emma needed and what Emma wanted was immeasurable.

Every few minutes he'd glance through the window as though he expected some divine intervention to have stopped the snowfall. Eventually she said, 'The best thing you can do is to put it out of your mind completely. The harder you will it to stop, the faster it will snow.'

The evening began to pick up momentum. Following some instinct she didn't care to investigate, she changed into a nicer dress and opened the Arpège sealed since Christmas. They ate and drank, managing to maintain between them a reasonable rally of comments pertaining to the ills endemic in the insides of motor cars.

'That was splendid.' David accepted more coffee. 'Per-

haps you should advertise meals for stranded travellers. I'm
sure you'd make a fortune.'

'There aren't many travellers to find themselves stranded.
My only neighbours are the farmer across the fields and the
funny farm up the road. Still, I suppose that's convenient
for the time when, driven mad with solitude, I run out
screaming into the highway.'

Under the influence of good food and a bottle of wine, it
seemed to him that her edges had softened. She sat, one
arm propped on the table, chin in hand, politely exhaling
smoke sideways. She's not all that bad-looking, he thought.
With a different hair-do and more feminine clothes, instead
of those straight-cut, no-nonsense efforts, she'd be quite
fancyable. Never make the lid of a chocolate box of course,
but there was, or could be, something quite striking. Not
often you saw that combination of red hair and brown eyes.
Odd really : a man and a woman thrust together for the
night in an isolated cottage; with anyone else he might be
weighing up the chances. Wonder if she's ever——? That
thought spawned another : Emma. Emma, presenting the
lineaments of gratified desire to another man, a man without
name, form or status, therefore that much more threatening.
To think of her was to invoke a pain like a band round his
head. Emma the unknowable, intangible, Emma the bitch.

'I should think they must be worth at least ten new
pennies.'

She'd been watching him for the past five minutes and
spoke so that he'd stop rattling his spoon round his saucer—
it was putting her teeth on edge.

'What?'

'Your thoughts.'

'I don't think you'd need to be much of a clairvoyant to
read them just now.'

'No, I suppose not.' She held her cigarette horizontally,

between finger and thumb, so that the smoke drifted in a perpendicular column, formed blue concentric rings, then dissolved. 'Do you love her very much?'

The question surprised her as much as it surprised him. It seemed as though it had escaped quite arbitrarily from her subconscious. She watched him deciding whether to use it as a springboard for rancour or as a chance to be honest. He chose honesty.

'I don't know whether I love her or I hate her. She's like a disease. Because she's never done this before, not to my knowledge anyway, it should make a difference, act as a . . .' He sought for the word.

'Catalyst?'

'Yes, that's it. But it doesn't. I mean, the situation's the same. The fact that she has someone else is the result of what's wrong rather than the cause of it.'

'And how long has it been—wrong?'

'It's been wrong for a long time. I should have thought you'd be able to tell me more than I know myself, you two being so close.'

'I don't think "close" is the right word. Anyway, when we talk, it's generally about the good old days gone by and how sweet we were—that sort of thing. Or about the success she's having with her drawing.'

'Her drawing, yes. I expect that's how she's come across this character—one of those flowery-tied drinkers of gin and tonic.'

She couldn't help laughing. 'Emma always did tend toward the flamboyant.'

'You've known her a long time, haven't you?'

'Ever since the days of Mickey Mouse gas masks and Beacon Readers. We went to the same schools, the same parties, persecuted each other in the same back gardens, we even ended up in the same town when I got my first job and she was in rep. Quixote and Sancho Panza—though I was never sure of the casting.'

'And having known her from cradle days, does that make her character crystal-clear to you?'

The brown eyes contemplated a spot on the opposite wall. 'Not really. While we were growing up, the necessary detachment was obscured by personal jealousies. And now, of course, age has taught discretion.'

She stood up and began to pile the plates together. Her briskness contrasted sharply with Emma's habitual drift. He was willing to bet that she'd been patrol-leader, form captain, head girl.

'Sit by the fire where it's comfortable. Shift the dog. I'll just clear these and then we'll have some whisky if you like.'

I can foresee, she thought, opening the kitchen door with her behind, us getting plastered and crying on each other's shoulders before the night's out and what started off as a Greek tragedy ending up as a Whitehall farce.

Patrick Derbyshire was a man of delicate sensibilities. Realizing the time had come when she needed to be alone to communicate with her husband, he excused himself and, in the public box in the hotel foyer, he made his own brief phone call. When lying had first become necessary, he'd been surprised at the facility with which he accomplished it, amazed at the sincerity in his voice as he manufactured meetings, dinners, unavoidable and long-drawn-out conferences. Sometimes he thought facetiously that he'd audition for the National Theatre, at other times he wondered, with a certain cool shiver, whether she, at loose among the white spaces of the empty house, was an actress of equal accomplishment, concealing the signs of gladness at his departure under a blanket of wifely patter about vests and toothpaste and liquor consumption.

Emma came into the bar, her face registering consecutive expressions of search, bewilderment, panic, then relief as he stepped out of the concealment of his niche.

'You have a habit of looking as though you expected me to have vanished during the briefest separation,' he said, putting her drink into her hand.

'That's how I feel. Even when you leave me to go to the loo, I'm frightened that you won't return.'

She had an irritating habit of raising the glass to her lips and setting it down again without drinking. There were so many endearing, irritating things he didn't know about her. She repeated the action twice, then turned to him.

'Patrick, there was no reply. I tried twice.'

'Something could have cropped up. Perhaps someone needed his returns fiddling at a moment's notice.'

But his attempt at humour fell on stony ground. Oh God, no, he thought, not an evening of worry and wondering. One of the essentials of an association like this was that the deceived should be granted a mention for form's sake, then pushed firmly back into their respective limbos.

'You can try again later. There are any number of things that could have called him out.'

What number of things? Cigarettes? He didn't smoke. An evening paper? He bought it on the way home from the station. A late meeting at the office? Unusual, but feasible. A drink with a colleague, because he had no reason to rush home? Bound to be one of those alternatives. Stupid to imagine that something had gone wrong.

Patrick drew on his cigarette and drank his whisky, waiting for her to come back to him as she was certain to do after her rapid conjecturing had led her to a comforting explanation. She might not admit it, or even know it, but her concern was basically for herself. He knew it from his own experience. The fear of being found out far outweighed the fear of domestic disaster.

'Let's eat.' A bottle of wine and a couple of brandies would put her right. First they'd get her talking, and the more she talked, the less she'd think, then she'd be ready for love and, locked together in the centre of the big bed, she'd forget the existence of the man David who might, or might not, have met with calamity.

Usually they managed to sit beside each other to eat, loath to miss any chance for their hands to brush or their knees to press, but tonight they faced each other across a snow-white sea of culinary barriers. He moved a pepper-pot, a table number, a small and delicate floral arrangement: 'I can't see you.'

'Don't you ever get tired of looking at my same old face?'

But she knew that that was one of the puzzling delights of early love. No matter how long and hard you looked, there were always fresh facets to discover, always an unsuspected line, a surprising curve. Love so altered your normal powers of observation that it was a face in a fog you saw which annoyingly refused to reassemble itself in the memory.

Across the table she took his hand, tracing bone and hair and muscle with her forefinger, looking at the ring with the green stone which held heaven-knew-what history. The waiter hovered, clearing his throat, waiting to put down their first courses. Not married, those two. He hoped they were staying in. If so, they'd be off to bed, leaving their gâteaux untouched and their coffee cups half-full. Otherwise they'd sit for hours, gazing into each other's eyes and you'd have to lift the table from between them before you'd get them to move.

Emma discarded the cherry, cracked the brown sugar and searched for a starting point in her grapefruit. She found the convention of shoving food down one's mouth at

socially regulated intervals an irritating one. In her art
school, bed-sitter days, she'd often worked until the giddi-
ness of hunger had brought her to a standstill. It seemed
far more logical to adjust one's eating habits to one's life
than vice versa.

'Look!' He indicated the couple at a neighbouring table,
chewing and swallowing, thoroughly and silently, physically
alike in the way that people long-married sometimes are.
'George and Margaret.'

'No! Norman and Dorothy. Definitely.'

'He's a freemason. They attend a great many dinner
dances where the women are all given to beaded evening
bags and drink Tia Maria.'

'That's right. Brethren! Please be upstanding for the
Worshipful Master. And the women all look alike because
they go to the same hairdresser. They wear brocade dresses
and have their shoes dyed to match, but they don't scrub
their backs often enough and there's always loose flesh on
the upper part of their arms.'

'He keeps girlie magazines locked in a drawer of his desk
at the office. He's very good about the house. She buys him
attachments for his drill as Christmas presents.'

'She belongs to the Townswomen's Guild and holds Con-
servative coffee mornings, while he potters in the garden
shed among the lengths of four-by-two.'

'She knits him fawn waistcoats and makes him wear
a vest. They have a son called Barry who's in the business
—they wish he'd get himself a nice girl-friend—and a
daughter called Denise who never washes off her eye
make-up and wants to be an actress. He has the most well-
polished car in the road and usually they go to Majorca for
their holidays, but this year it's going to be a cruise to the
Canary Islands.'

It was a game they often played. People were so **predict-**

ably awful. She waited until the waiter had moved away, then said, 'I know as much about them as I do about you.'

'I hope not.'

'It's true.'

'What do you want to know?' He sawed at his steak, grinning. 'I was born in 1933 at a place called Wick, which is up there.' He stabbed the air above her head with his finger. 'I have one older sister and one younger brother, one who tormented me and the other who was tormented by me. My father's a retired solicitor and my mother breeds dogs. I am married with one son aged ten. My blood group is "O" and I like my eggs turned and fried hard. How will that do?'

She had on her bear-with-him face. 'Well, it's mutual,' he said. 'What do I know about your murky past? You wet the bed and sucked your thumb. You loved your father and hated your mother. Or you loved your mother and hated your father. What does it matter?'

'It shouldn't, but it does. Knowing all those things makes up, in part, for all the years we spent finding each other. And surely, all the episodes in our past have formed us into our present selves. Or have they?'

'You mean, do events shape us, or we them, precisely because we are what we are and therefore set those events in motion? I don't know. But I think I incline to the latter view. Drink your wine. I didn't pick you because I suspected you had hidden depths of philosophical reasoning.'

'Then why did you?'

'Because you're a dishy bird.'

'And you're a coarse-grained adulterer.'

'And you're a loose woman. And we'll both be turned away from the pearly gates. Have some Charlotte Russe.'

'No, thank you. Loose women can't afford to lose their waistlines.'

She smiled at him. 'Isn't it curious that whenever I know we're going to meet, I imagine that our time together will be sad and soul-searching. But it's never like that. You make me laugh, liberate me from all my dark, female suspicions.'

So, she sat at home, thinking nervously of the women who, by mere accident of profession, saw more of him than she did, wondering perhaps whether she was only one of any number of spare-time liaisons. Surely she could envisage the purely practical difficulties of carrying on like that? Anyway, he had reached that age when lust is not enough.

Blue-rimmed coffee cup in her hand, alternately blowing and sipping, how remote she could look. Black dress, black hair, washed-out blue eyes, the personification of enigma. He had to remove the mask, to uncover her, to penetrate deeper and deeper to the core of her in the only way he knew.

'Let's go,' he said. And, unknown to them, two people waiting in the lounge got a table rather sooner than they'd expected.

Jacket, pants, tie, cuff-links, bath, toothbrush, impatience, Emma unnecessarily pulling a minuscule white lace garment over her head, windows curtained, door locked, radio playing something suitably muted, towelling himself dry and razoring himself smooth, patting on exotic Christmas present lotion for her and pausing a moment before touching her, blue eyes huge and drowning him, the slope of her shoulder and curve of her back, their names in each other's mouth, wondrous syllables, uttered involuntarily, but seeming to sum up taste and sensation and need in two words. Her skin warm and cool, satin and alabaster, poet's words, her hands gentle and knowing, drawing separate currents of desire into one channel. Until the very last moment, concerned for him more than for herself, then feeling her nails grazing his back and looking down triumphantly into those eyes now unseeing, totally surrendered, her cry merging into the finale of a piano concerto. In the silence, he remained, breathing hair, fragrance and sweat, delaying the tiny trauma of parting, waiting for his consciousness to re-focus itself.

Her hand moved to his neck, combing and re-combing a tangle of curls, tracing the curve of an ear-lobe. This was the time when she wanted to say all those foolish, true, conventional things she was not authorized to say. Oh to be a man and confine your emotions to the appropriate physical area.

He lit a cigarette, drew on it and held it between her lips. 'You were lovely.'

'Only because of you. And to think.' She couldn't suppress the thought. 'At this very moment, I should be engaged in innocent girlish chatter. Not lying replete in the arms of a lover.'

'Oh yes, the formidable Geraldine. Quite the *fidus Achates*, isn't she? I thought that such loyalty was found only among men. Does she get some sort of kick out of it?'

'Geraldine always gives me the impression that she'd regard carnal love as something messy and rather pointless and suitable for dogs.'

He fitted her into his side and settled the sheet around them. 'Then the formidable Geraldine doesn't know what she's missing.'

With a last spiteful flurry, the snow had moved on to plague another part of the country, giving place to a wind which, with banshee wails, threatened to take the slates off the roof. 'Souls in torment,' Geraldine said. 'There's something about the architecture of this house which distils a fearsome moan from the gentlest gust.'

The fire was banked up, the level inside the whisky bottle

was falling steadily, she was grateful for the bulk of man-
hood which sat comfortably between her and the fantasies
engendered by the elemental fury. She'd discovered her
fears about the evening to be unfounded. In fact, it was
quite refreshing to talk to someone who didn't interrupt your
own eloquent stream every few minutes to steer the conversation along his own channels. Or maybe it was just the
whisky.

She'd been telling him about the dame school which she
and Emma had attended: white panamas with brown
bands, cups of dusty hot milk handed round at break-time
by the faltering Miss Macdonald, each one accompanied by
a maxim for the day: 'What a tangled web we weave when
first we practise to deceive.' Then a steady walk in twos
round the garden and back to the classroom and the malicious ruler of the robust Miss Macdonald. 'We were taught
the accomplishments of ladies, all very low key, embroidery
and the piano, recitation and some sweet pastoral warblings.
Did you know that ladies walk differently and absolutely
never cross their legs when sitting down?'

'You speak of it with affection.'

'I liked the ordered routine of school. You knew where
you were. If everything else had been as clear-cut as school,
I'd have been a lot happier.'

'Somehow I can't imagine you two in gymslips, trailing
your satchels in the dust,' he said.

'Nor can I, for the main part. Only odd, vividly-coloured
incidents stand out. I remember the Wednesdays though.'

'Why the Wednesdays?'

'Because Wednesdays were music lessons followed by tea
at Emma's. Arranged by our parents of course. Whether we
were speaking or not speaking, it was a ritual: on Saturdays
Emma came to tea and on Wednesdays I went to tea at
Emma's.'

71

And there were so many times when they weren't speaking. Staring into the fire, the scents and sounds of a May afternoon mingled with a sudden visual image. The reason why they weren't speaking, not surprisingly, escaped her. One of those petty crimes, no doubt, that are heinous in the eyes of a child. She smelt again the dank cloakroom where she and Emma stood apart from each other—though their pegs were adjacent—buttoning brown blazers and lacing brown shoes. 'Your badge is crooked.' This triumphant information, imparted through clenched teeth, was ignored by Geraldine who, garments askew and bag swinging belligerently from one bony shoulder, strode up the stone steps and out of the building. Her one advantage was that she could always leave Emma behind. Already, at ten, Geraldine towered above her classmates, surreptitiously pulling down her skirt in an attempt to cover the ever-increasing gap between hem and knee. Parents noticed her as the child with the ferocious expression who stood in the centre of the back row at end-of-term concerts. 'You're a freak,' Emma said. 'You're nearly as tall as my father.' It was patently untrue, but had been responsible for the stoop which characterized her adolescent years.

On a perfect May afternoon as eulogized by madrigal singers, separated by fifty yards, they had trod through the fallen petals of Japanese cherry blossoms, each dragging her steps as the destination loomed nearer.

'Come on. Come *on*.' At the gate of number fifty-three, Geraldine tapped her foot and tossed her head, but not one pace faster moved the other child's feet. She wouldn't have done any practice either. Only did occasionally, then played like an angel, showing off, all ringlets and white silk socks.

Geraldine's gloomy predictions were fulfilled : Emma had not practised. In Miss H. V. Kershaw's sitting-room, surrounded by chintz and sepia photographs of Father and

Uncle Wilfrid going off to fight the Hun, Emma was a positive fund of wrong notes, for which, as Geraldine had foreseen, they both suffered. Oblivious to the tick of the metronome, the rhythmic tap of the pencil, the Marche Militaire stumbled along and finally petered out entirely. 'Stop, stop!' Miss H. V. Kershaw, who still cherished fantasies of the drama of the concert platform, ran a delicate hand across a cultured brow. 'There are two weeks left before the concert. Your timing is terrible and neither of you seems to be able to distinguish a crotchet from a quaver. Stop smirking Emma. It's nothing to be proud of. Let's try again.'

Old ratbag, Emma thought. And just look at Geraldine's chamber-pot face. Worth playing badly—it put her off. Serve her right. Practising every night in that awful room above the P.G.s' lounge, just so that she'll be better than me.

How can anyone be expected to play properly against that? Geraldine tried to close her ears to the distracting errors being perpetrated in the treble clef. It's unfair. Why can't we have separate lessons? Why do people think we're friends? I hate Emma. I'd like to hang Emma and see her face go purple and her eyes bulge out.

Two tiresome little girls. Helen Kershaw closed her eyes and felt the late-afternoon sun on her cheek. Sometimes she could almost believe that Emma deliberately played badly. And the other one was so consistently sullen. It wouldn't do. If there was no improvement by next week, their parents would have to be informed that their lessons were a waste of time.

'D'you think she will?' Standing outside in the waste of crazy paving that made up the front garden, Geraldine was willing to bury a temporary hatchet in the face of this new threat.

'She's too poor.'

'Is she?' Geraldine searched her terms of reference. Poor was the children who lived in the houses by the canal where she was forbidden to play, the children whose clothes were too big or too small, who threw stones and shouted rude words. None of these designations fitted Miss Kershaw, who drank tea from a fluted gold and white cup and cut the angel cake with a silver-handled knife.

'You're quite poor too, aren't you?' Sly-eyed Emma, arching her dancing feet on the paving stones, pointed pink tongue caught between sharp white teeth. 'Or you wouldn't have to take P.G.s.'

'We are not!' Pale, freckled skin suffused with rose. She'd *kill* Emma. But Emma had skipped out of range. 'If you're *coming* to tea, you'd better come on. But I shan't speak to you.'

And she didn't . . .

'Wake up!'

Geraldine started, saw David and came back to earth. 'I'm sorry. I was day-dreaming.'

'You were in a trance.'

'I was remembering my youth and realizing that we change less than we'd like to think we do.'

'How very profound. Which particular bit of your youth prompted that realization?'

She smiled. 'I was remembering how, although we continually insulted and abused one another, Emma and I stuck together. I think our respective homes were the attraction. She liked mine because it was always full of activity and people ready to make a fuss of her. I liked hers because—well, you remember Emma's home—it gave me a glimpse of the gracious living I knew must exist somewhere.'

'I was only there twice before they moved. But I remember that it was very beautiful and that they had a maid and a housekeeper and that I was petrified I'd use the wrong fork or turn round too quickly and smash something.'

'It seemed to me, as a child, that entering that household demanded the same sort of deliberate expunging of frivolity that was necessary before you could enter church. Emma would pitch her satchel into a cupboard and disappear and I'd stand stock-still in the middle of that endless expanse of parquet, listening to various clocks ticking in various rooms, smelling flowers and polish and quiet, just savouring the stillness. Mrs Sainter would be lying down—I could never understand why anyone should need that amount of lying down. I always thought of her as some shadowy Lady of Shalott, making paces about her curtained room and occasionally raising a pre-Raphaelite hand to the loom. There was a picture of her in the hall, painted when she was a young girl; it used to fill me with a peculiar melancholy—to know that once she must have been vivid and laughing and in love with life.'

'The first time *I* met her was the most eerie experience of my life. I was sitting in the breakfast-room waiting for Emma to come down, when her mother came in through one door, talking quietly to herself, saw me, smiled, and went out through the other, still talking. Emma told me afterwards that it was one of her bad days.'

'They were few and far between, you know. Most of the time she was all right—vague, but all right. It was him I felt sorry for. He had such a capacity for enjoyment.'

'And from all accounts,' David said, 'he spent the greater part of his time satisfying it.'

'You make him sound like some old roué. He wasn't at all like that. He was kind and considerate and so attractive, in that pensive way, that my stomach used to turn over when he came into the room.'

She remembered him : standing in a doorway, starched

white shirt and city suit, blue eyes and laughter lines, as beautiful and inaccessible as the men in the books.

'He always struck me as a man whose charm concealed weakness—' He broke off and looked at her and they were both aware that he'd used the wrong tense.

'If he *does* die,' Geraldine said, 'she'll never forgive herself.'

David was silent. How curious it was, he thought, that the person Emma undoubtedly loved best in the world, should have been the unwitting cause of her betrayal.

'I was a pampered only child,' Emma said, curling strands of his luxuriant chest hair around her fingers.

Or a neglected one, Patrick wondered, judging by what little he knew of her family background; the ailing mother, the father involved with another woman.

Neither of them had the inclination for sleep. The radio was switched low and to a background of old-time dancing from the Locarno ballroom, they stroked and kissed and talked.

'You never talk of your mother,' he said. 'Always your father.'

She hesitated. 'My mother is what kind people describe as "not quite the thing"—it isn't the sort of information you want to broadcast.' Seeing his face, she added quickly, 'She's not in a padded cell, if that's what you're thinking. I believe the medical term is chronic depression. She's just—withdrawn and has days when she gets the past mixed up with the present. I had a brother who died in infancy after an accident and I believe she held herself totally responsible. She started to be ill soon after. I never realized it for years of course. She'd spend days in bed, but I thought she had some genuine disability. I remember one day at school— we were reading *Jane Eyre* and we'd reached the part

where Mrs Rochester is introduced—I overheard someone
whispering "That's like Emma Sainter's mother".'

'God.' He pulled her closer to him, as if attempting to
erase those brutal childish words of long ago.

'So you see why Flora, and the others, were inevitable.
Why I can't blame him. Some men would have taken to
drink or buried themselves in their work, but he's always
been the sort of man women find attractive. Even the formidable Geraldine had a crush on him.'

'Poor Emma,' he said. 'It sounds as though you had a
rough time. Weren't you jealous?'

'Of Flora? Never. She wasn't competing, she couldn't
have stolen him from me. Of Geraldine, funnily enough,
yes. She had no right to regard my father as something
special. That was my prerogative. And what a little bitch I
was. It makes me shudder to remember. I deliberately
arranged it that her illusions should be shattered in the most
painful way.'

'You're invited to dinner tomorrow night,' she'd said.
'You, me, Papa and Flora. Liar that I am, I said that I
wouldn't enjoy it unless you came too. It's an end-of-
term treat. It'll be somewhere posh, so for God's sake try to
look decent.'

'Who's Flora?' Geraldine had said, laying aside the *Odes*
of Horace and wondering how she could possibly contain
herself until tomorrow night.

'Who's Flora indeed!' Emma, infuriating as always,
merely swung her lissom, lisle-clad legs over the back of a
desk and adopted her Greta Garbo expression.

Expecting the worst, knowing that clothes and Geraldine
seemed to have no more than a passing affinity, Emma,
riffling through the lodgers' letters on the table in Geraldine's hall while she waited, was agreeably surprised.

'Do stop staring.' Having turned out and surveyed the

whole of her not-extensive wardrobe for the occasion, Geraldine felt entitled to be prickly.

'You look OK. Except for your mother's lipstick.'

'It's not my mother's lipstick.'

'It might just as well be. Puce! You look like a harlot.' It was a relatively new word to her vocabulary and one that she used indiscriminately.

In the bus, Geraldine, having resolutely refused to remedy the offending puce, tried, in a subtle fashion, to catch glimpses of herself in the window to see if it still looked as glamorous as when she'd put it on. Emma did the same, but less subtly, confident that the reflection would be pleasing.

She wondered if they'd get drinks. Or would all their painting and powdering and attempts to add four years to their age end up in the indignity of two fizzy lemonades with straws? Flora, of course, wouldn't make the mistake of treating her like a child, but her father, in matters pertaining to her age, could be surprisingly obtuse.

Past the commissionaire, up in a lift, along corridors and through archways, she led Geraldine, into the very heart of the immense grey Gothic building where Robert Sainter controlled a not too modest empire. Aspiring employees saluted her, deferential secretaries called her Miss Sainter—she accepted it all with aplomb. She did not find it at all surprising that her father should be something special to these people too.

'We need a ball of twine,' Geraldine said, 'like Theseus in the labyrinth.'

Geraldine was overawed. Geraldine's voice was trembling. How strange to be Geraldine, to feel your knees shaking and your pulse racing at the prospect of seeing one's father. Still, this should make her realize the pointlessness of her passion. They knocked and entered.

One day, Emma thought, I shall look like Flora. One day,

after much trial and error, I'll learn to wear a simple, elegant grey suit like that, with just one silver brooch pinned to the lapel and how to put on just the right amount of make-up and have my hair cut so it looks like a piece of black silk. One day, *I'll* be a personal assistant to some gorgeous, dishy man like my father. Except that of course I don't suppose there are many gorgeous, dishy men just like my father.

Robert Sainter looked from one youthful face to the other, with amusement. They looked a little like those painted child prostitutes he'd seen in Cairo. If they'd been alone, he'd have ordered Emma to wipe it off immediately, thought its effect on her was not quite so disastrous as upon Geraldine. Emma, of course, had not been able to resist telling him, with a certain giggling malice, that poor little Geraldine was eating her heart out (Wasn't it killing? A hoot). And, sensitive though he was, the inevitable blinkers of maturity made it impossible for him to imagine it as anything deeper than a three-week divertissement conceived out of midsummer boredom. A pity all the same. And Emma, warned though she might be, could be relied upon not to ease the death pangs. Sometimes he noticed a certain sharp look in Emma's eyes which disturbed him. Perhaps his policy of openness had been a mistake. Perhaps she was old enough to put two and two together and reach the conclusion that he was not just a parent, after all, but a man as well.

Flora was marvellous. He realized it, Geraldine realized it, Emma thought: She's so knowing, so cool, so everything I want to be, that I should feel jealous, but I don't. Through the daunting sequence of knives and forks and waiters and wines she led them with a touch that was never less than light and graceful. They sipped tall, frothy drinks called Pussyfoots, feeling bold, and unaware that they were as lacking in alcohol as the despised lemonade; they were drawn out to talk upon subjects other than the hated ritual of how was school and which exams they were taking; when Emma looked pointedly at a small silver cigarette case, she was included in the invitation and then courteously ignored when, after two puffs, she had to let the cigarette burn itself out in the ashtray. Blue eyes and brown eyes surveyed thick carpet, crystal chandelier and the long-necked, frosted elegance of wine bottles and wondered how soon it would be before they could claim this muted sophistication as their right.

He can bring her here, Emma thought, because he's got us two as an alibi. But I bet they usually have to search out country pubs and outlying restaurants for their meetings. Except, of course, when he parks his car round some inconspicuous corner and visits her flat. And then? She thought of Rodin statues and gradually found it less difficult to visualize him in another role than the one of a husband who slept in a different bedroom from his wife. Having accepted that, she was surprised at her lack of reaction, one way or the other. Repugnance, jealousy, even prurient fascination, failed to manifest themselves. He was her father and though Flora might occupy the periphery of his life, the centre of it was her territory and would remain so. She looked across the table at silly, innocent Geraldine, too innocent and insulated by adoration to realize the truth of the situation.

They travelled back on the bus because he and Flora had to meet an important client for after-dinner drinks.

'And that's what's known as a tissue of lies,' Emma said, making eyes at the conductor so they'd get away with half-fare.

'What do you mean?' Geraldine, eyes shining, was inhabiting a world where Emma's mother died painlessly in

a sanatorium and she became the second Mrs Sainter in a
flurry of grey top hats and camellias.

'They'll be going back to her flat for an evening of
passion.' Emma stressed the sibilants with unnecessary
emphasis.

'Why do you always think the worst, Emma?'

'Oh Geraldine!' Impatient set of the mouth, click of the
fingers. 'Do grow up. It's as plain as day. They're having an
affair. They're lovers. They go to bed together.'

And looking into Geraldine's eyes in which painful comprehension was gradually dawning, she experienced an
exhilaration that was only just tinged with shame.

Sixteen years later, Emma clutched at the hand of her
lover and said, to his astonishment, 'But I'm nicer now,
surely? I must be nicer now.'

I am really rather drunk. Geraldine giggled and then
flinched as she poured boiling water over the rim of the
mug and dangerously near her free hand. And it seems as
though I've rather lost the knack of it. It's a long time since I
was drunk proper.

With exaggerated care, she picked up the two black
coffees and carried them out of the kitchen. David's large
outstretched hand seemed a long way off and it demanded
an enormous amount of concentration for her to guide the
mug into it. She took great scalding mouthfuls and felt her
swimming vision begin to reorientate itself.

'I think you're a bit tight.'

'Mm.'

'So am I,' he said. 'Under the circumstances, I think it's
the best way to be. Everything seems so much simpler.
Warm fire, pleasant surroundings, oblivion of the grain.
What more can one ask?'

He certainly was tight. Oblivion of the grain indeed! And

when, waving a hand at the evidence of her domestic skills, he said, 'I can't understand why you're not married,' she groaned inwardly. Wasn't that the customary gambit of men experiencing the frisky courage of inebriation? Now that *would* be divine justice. Emma returning, face wiped free of ecstasy, to discover that the gulled husband and the ever-faithful friend had used the source of their common interest as an excuse to find solace in bed together.

In her best, clipped, schoolmarm tones (or the nearest approximation she could manage, with half a bottle of wine and seven whiskies inside her) she said, 'Perhaps the right man got away, or never came along, or doesn't exist. Or perhaps I'm just not cut out for it. Any one of those reasons will do.' They'll do for me, she thought, so I'm sure they'll do for you.

'The ones who get away aren't usually the right ones, are they?'

'Equally so, the ones who don't get away aren't always the right ones. Have you never wondered whether the somebody you didn't marry might have been the one you should have married?'

'Often.' He rocked to and fro, nursing his coffee cup. He had one of those slow, sweet smiles which, for the space of its existence, can transform the merely attractive into the beautiful. 'I was engaged to a girl once. She worked in the library. We used to save a mutual four pounds a week in the Burnley Building Society to put towards a house—and that entailed me cutting out cigarettes and her setting her own hair and cycling to work. Then Emma came along.'

'Emma had a genius for coming along at the wrong moment. There have been times in my life when I'd have been spared a lot of misery if Emma hadn't come along at the wrong moment.'

'Why? What did she do? Waltz off with your childhood sweetheart?'

'Yes,' she said simply. And he reflected that every glib little phrase wounded somebody.

'I was very jealous of Emma.'

'Jealous?' He seemed genuinely astonished. 'Because she's good-looking? But she's unhappy. I expect she will always be unhappy. Emma doesn't seem to have the talent for happiness. You're not like that. You have too much good sense to cultivate unhappiness. Surely?'

'How on earth can you say that? You don't know me.'

'No. But I've found that first impressions usually contain a germ of truth because that's the only time they're purely objective. I remember seeing you at that party, looking bored but brave, and thinking: "At last a human being".'

'Not so much bored as completely out of my depth among all those professional charmers.'

She'd been press-ganged into that party—'Why don't you go out and have some fun?' Emma had said so often until at last she'd capitulated, gone to the wretched party and hated every minute of it. Her first and last excursion into Emma's theatrical milieu.

'I felt the same way,' he said. 'They were the kind of people who had to be sure you were worth talking to before they'd make the effort. My passport to inclusion was Emma. Otherwise I'd have been just another boring, conventionally-suited, grey person.'

She laughed. 'They did go on so about grey people, didn't they? I could never grasp their fine distinctions.'

'You wore a brown frock and a gold necklace.'

'And you went to find me some beer because I just couldn't face any more of that dreadful draught red wine everyone else was drinking. You said, "I wonder how soon one could decently leave?" When you came back, Emma grabbed you to dance and I didn't see you again. Some girl with silver hair got paralytic and started to take off her clothes.'

'God yes! She'd had her appendix removed at some stage I remember. I was terribly embarrassed. Emma said she was mixing up work with leisure.'

'A funny little man in a torn green shirt took me home in a taxi, borrowed the fare, then tried to rape me on the doorstep.'

She emptied the dregs of the whisky into his glass. 'At the time, I felt that it was me who was out-of-step. Because, after all, those were the kind of crazy things one was supposed to enjoy in one's light-hearted youth. I just didn't have the knack.'

'If you were out-of-step, then so was I. It wasn't us Geraldine. It was them. They were phoney and they were dangerous and if I'd had an atom of sense, I'd have rushed right back to my librarian whose demand for pleasure ran no higher than two back-row seats in the stalls and a box of Black Magic.'

She looked at him squarely. 'You don't mean that.'

'I didn't know my priorities then. I do now. Then, I couldn't distinguish surface glitter from value. Now perhaps I'm a little more capable of doing so. Socially, temperamentally, Emma and I were at opposite ends of the spectrum. I thought, in my innocence, that those things didn't matter. They do.'

'Socially?'

'Oh I know—I don't drop my aitches or cover my walls with plaster ducks—but all the same, I don't have that air of supreme invulnerability possessed by those who are born rich or aristocratic. And it's that kind of strength and command that Emma admires most of all. She thinks weakness is despicable and she can't love what she despises.'

Then she must despise me, Geraldine thought, because as far as she's concerned, I've been weak all along the line. Right from the time when she used to con me into doing her homework, up to now, when she uses me as a confederate. When I was seventeen I fell madly in love with a small, fair-haired boy called Howard and then watched as Emma stole him from me, not because she wanted him for herself particularly, just because she was bored and needed to keep her hand in. Why have we remained friends? I suppose it's because I still regard her as a wilful child and you can't judge children by adult standards.

She looked across at David. His eyes were closing and his tie was left of centre. There were new lines in his face since last she'd seen him. You should have clung to your irreproachable library girl, she thought. You'd have had three sturdy imperturbable children by now, a pleasant, unpretentious home and a smooth forehead. Working-class boy made good, who could blame you for your aspirations? How could you have been expected to know that the transition from a Smethwick terraced-house and the girl next door to a white and desirable residence beside the Thames with a beautiful wife would demand such a sacrifice of tranquillity?

As she reached across to take his glass, he stirred and blinked and sat up. 'Gosh I'm sorry. I don't usually fall asleep in the middle of conversations. It's just that today's been exhausting, in every respect.'

'I've made up the bed in the spare room.'

Their eyes collided, flickered for an instant, then shifted again. 'Yes,' he said. 'I suppose I'd better turn in. Tomorrow's going to be a big day.' He stood up. 'You don't suppose there's the remotest chance that tomorrow won't come?'

'When I was a child,' she said, 'I used to close my eyes all the way to the dentist, believing that what I didn't see, couldn't exist. But I felt the drill in my mouth all the same, and it was that much more horrible because I hadn't prepared myself for it.'

'I'd guessed that you were a Girl Guide,' he said, with a wan attempt at humour.

And she wondered why it should be that she was so much better at organizing other people's lives than organizing her own.

'I know that by staying awake we seem to be delaying the progress of time's winged chariot, but I really must get some kip or I'll be dead in the morning. If I snore, turn me over. It's the only thing that works.'

Patrick kissed her temple, turned from her, and within minutes was sleeping the deep, motionless sleep of the physically exhausted, while Emma fitted herself into the curves of his back and prepared herself for several long, dark, wakeful hours.

Those casual, thoughtless statements of his: 'Turn me over. It's the only thing that works,' stabbed her, evoking as they did the image of a faceless woman who washed his socks, knew how many minutes to boil his eggs, was familiar with his coughs and snores and had carried his child inside her body. Right at the beginning Emma had told herself that jealousy, as well as being destructive, would also be profitless—he wouldn't leave bloody sacrosanct Beryl, whatever happened. Nevertheless, there was nothing she could do to prevent these occasional excruciating reminders of her precarious position. Jealousy was demeaning. It implied one's own inferiority. It was only now she could understand why, for three months in 1957, Geraldine had refused to speak to her. Short, fair-haired boy. What was his name?

Began with a G. Gordon? Graham? Howard! That was it.
What a bore he'd turned out to be. Just Geraldine's type in
fact: earnest and scholarly. It had been a low trick of
course. But then everything had been so morbid that winter
and, at first glance, he had looked like the Apollo Belvedere.
And surely, if he'd been *that* keen on Geraldine, he wouldn't
have changed his affections. Besides, she had to admit it,
there'd been a certain kick in taking Geraldine down one
enormous peg: the cleverest and most reliable girl in the
class, always the one to stay behind and water the damned
broad beans on blotting paper or something, everybody's
favourite girl. It had been really quite sickening.

She glanced across the dark hump of bedclothes that was
Patrick to the illuminated dial of his watch on the bedside
table. Only three o'clock. It couldn't be possible. Beside the
gentle, rhythmic movement of his back, she tossed and
turned. It was always the same: an unfamiliar body, a certain amount of drink, over-excitement, and insomnia was
inevitable. It would be unfair to wake him. He'd spent
himself for her sake as well as his own. Funny really, she'd
never been that keen on it before she met him. She'd
regarded it as just an inevitable step to something else—
something indefinable. It was only with him she'd come to
think of the act of love as an activity that could be complete
in itself. Maybe that was lowering it to an animal level, but
then animals weren't neurotic, were they? Really it was
very funny when she remembered that at art school, she was
considered to be the most sexually experienced girl of her
year. Of course, it was mainly because she had a positive
genius for getting herself into compromising situations.
Actually it had been quite a useful reputation—every one
of them had thought she was having it off with one of the
others and so refrained from pestering her. Another funny
thing was that, in fact, it seemed more than likely that

Geraldine had been initiated first, all among the dreaming spires at that.

Leaving home, breaking the cord, losing one's virginity—the order of things. Waiting for the dawn to break—did dawn actually break in February?—she remembered that July afternoon, in the same year as the Howard incident, when she'd sat, with others not sufficiently mature to be made prefects, at the back of the school assembly hall, passing Polo mints and scurrilous comments about Viscountess X who was presenting the prizes, while Geraldine, straight and severe, as befitted the head girl, received a perfect library of leather-bound collected works. Their last days of security. In three months their paths were to diverge: Emma's leading to London and Life, Geraldine's steps bound for the groves of Lady Margaret Hall. Both, at that stage, were anxious to be off; it was not until the first few desolate weeks that they reached for pen and paper, wrote long, desperate letters to each other, tore them up and began again: 'It's absolutely great here. Free at last! I'm going to a dance tonight and tomorrow there's a debate.' Eventually the letters became true and therefore less frequent.

There was hope for us then, Emma thought. Then, when we were ready and willing to assimilate anything and everything, when we were still able to believe that we were each too special for fate to deny us an illustrious future: me, playing at *la vie Bohème*, Geraldine falling in love with that terribly self-assured young don, walking about dazed, unable to think of anything but bridesmaids' dresses and baguette-cut diamonds.

She folded an arm round Patrick and began to stroke his chest, but the response was nil, so turning back to her own half of the bed, she abandoned herself to wholehearted three o'clock nostalgia.

That second summer away from home, Emma had welcomed an invitation to Oxford. London was marvellous of course, but the frantic tempo it was necessary to maintain in order not to be excluded from anything tended to be fatiguing.

'Geraldine!'

Geraldine, waiting at the station barrier, had failed to recognize the new Emma. Straight black hair had been allowed to grow to shoulder-blade length and fell heavy each side of a pale, pale face dominated by eyes enormous with blacking. 'Shrink your jeans in the bath,' someone had said and the result of the experiment was a heavy cold and a pair of the tightest jeans in living history. On one of the hottest days of the year—the tar was bubbling on the roads —Emma wore a long, thick, black jersey that must have been knitted on tent poles and which gave off a mingled odour of smoke, turpentine and something much more unpleasant.

'Aren't you rather warm?' Geraldine herself was wearing a sleeveless cotton dress with a low neckline, above the rim of which was to be seen a fair expanse of heavily freckled chest.

'Oh this?' Emma tugged at the jersey until it covered her knees and swung the B.O.A.C. bag, her only item of luggage, over her shoulder. 'I think it belongs to Sebastian. I found it in the casting-room. Somebody big anyway.'

She saw Geraldine looking at her with a look that said, 'I suspect that your appearance is a deliberate charade, thought up specially for the occasion.' And Geraldine wasn't far off the mark either. Emma, whose usual mode of dress was slightly more restrained, spurred on by images of cross-eyed intellectuals in pale blue twin-sets and flat shoes, had worked with industry to assemble a picture of artistic decadence.

They walked down the hill, chattering about trains and exams and accommodation. Geraldine had changed; it was more obvious seeing her in her natural setting. She looked less—angular, not fatter, but as though something had rounded off the corners. Even in that awful flowered frock and the hairstyle which seemed to have been fashioned purely for the sake of neatness, she conveyed a certain, unusual, aura of feminine bloom.

Even so, Dennis came as a surprise. Particularly after that ghastly all-girls-together bit in Hall.

Women, women everywhere—and mostly ugly women at that. Women were bad enough singularly, but en masse—! School all over again. Scrubbed cheeks and enthusiasm. Just one or two, cool and glam, who looked as though they might have things on their mind other than Anglo-Saxon studies and the hockey team. Emma was in her role of patronizingly amused audience at a raree show. Thank God she'd 'showed promise but never applied herself seriously enough' if this is how she'd have ended up. Funnily enough, Gerry, who used to be dangerously like this when they were at school, seemed to have taken a turn for the better. Perhaps she'd snatched a glance at those desiccated old bats of lady dons and seen the light. Emma ate her dinner, surveyed her companions and wondered what on earth Sid, or Sebastian, or any other of her disreputable retinue would make of it all.

They were going to visit Dennis. That was his name, the Man, who'd rounded off Geraldine's corners, Dennis. Emma changed back from her borrowed dress to jeans and sweater and, when she met him, regretted it immediately. She'd been prepared for some woolly scholar in wide flannel pants. When he opened the door her mouth almost dropped open in shock. Hair, eyes, profile—the lot. And over his shoulder in the mirror at the end of the hall, she caught her reflection : she looked like a cross between a builder's labourer and a Romany refugee.

He was very polite, but she hadn't missed his initial look of astonishment. Sitting cross-legged among his collection of highbrow records and recondite literature, she felt childish, scruffy and absurd and, above all, surprised by her immediate intuitive certainty that he and Geraldine were lovers.

But, oh Geraldine, you're overdoing it a bit you know, she thought. You haven't read nearly enough women's magazines. The quickest way to frighten a man off is to smother him with adoration. Certainly he's a catch, and granted your experience in this field is somewhat limited, but cool it down or he'll move on to a bigger challenge. From the time they'd arrived, Geraldine's eyes hadn't left his face; she'd followed him into the kitchen when he went for glasses; if he hadn't stated his destination towards the end of the evening she'd have followed him into the loo. Had Emma been the sort of girl to give advice, she'd have said, 'Slow the pace, cast your net wider, hide your yearning behind an enormous pair of mental sunglasses.' But, being Emma, who would no more have given advice than have expected to receive it, she said nothing and was therefore not unduly surprised when she learned, in the fullness of time, that the grand passion had been consumed by that which had nourished it.

Geraldine lay in a foetal position, seeking warmth. Through the bedroom wall, she could hear the noisy insufflations and whistling exclamations that were David at slumber. Insomnia was just about supportable if you were alone; being tantalized by the audible evidence of somebody else's ability to sleep was not. She stuck it for twenty minutes, then switched on the light and opened the drawer where the sleeping tablets were kept. 'You shouldn't need these,' the doctor had said. 'Plenty of fresh air and exercise. Head buried in the books too much, is it?' He was a doctor of the old school: as long as your bowels were functioning, there couldn't be much wrong with you. She'd felt ashamed, as though she were an addict begging for heroin.

Julia Sainter lived on pills: pills to put her to sleep and pills to wake her up again. Geraldine had often accompanied Emma to the chemist to change the prescriptions. Pink pills in the evenings and white ones in the mornings. Once, Emma, thwarted in some design and feeling dramatic, had flushed half a bottle of the pink ones down the lavatory and then feigned coma. The doctor on that occasion, also one of the old school, had said, with a grim expression, that what she needed was a good walloping, while Robert Sainter stroked her forehead, Julia wrung her hands and Geraldine, carrying a message from school, sat downstairs in the hall wondering if she'd have to buy black clothes.

She screwed the top on the bottle and put it back in the drawer. Accepting the easy way out, even if it happened to be the right way, had never been her disposition.

She went quietly downstairs, Pinkerton yawning and thudding down, step by step, behind her. The fire was still glowing. She put on more coal and pulled her chair close to it. Often she found it easier to fall asleep in a chair by the fireside. How could David sleep so soundly? The drink, she supposed. She was feeling completely sober. She could drink most people under the table, and without after-effects either. It was something she was curiously proud about. Of course it meant too that the dulling of troublesome thoughts was that much more difficult. Watching the clock and drawing on cigarette after cigarette, troublesome thoughts seemed determined to intrude themselves upon her consciousness. It was this sudden turn of other people's events, she knew, that was forcing her into unwilling assessment of her own situation. All very well to look at a mockery of a marriage like David and Emma's and consider herself well out of it, but the fact remained, she was thirty-one and she had no man to keep her warm at night.

Just as well that she was a school-teacher. There was still the old idea in certain people's minds that women either got married or opted for the path of higher learning. At least it saved her from a few of those 'And when are the wedding bells going to ring for you Geraldine?' types of comment.

Even Emma, deliberate spurner of the conventions, was surprisingly realistic on the subject: 'Oh, I know I'm no advertisement for marriage, but it is comforting to know that there's always somebody there, even if it's only to bring you tea in bed when you've got the 'flu. Think what it must be like to be sixty-five or something and know there's nobody in the world who gives a damn about you. Even if your life-partner happens to detest you, at least it's a positive reaction.'

'Shouldn't love enter into things somewhere along the line?' Geraldine had asked.

'Love? Ask me that in twenty-five years' time when I've found out what the word means.'

'You see,' Geraldine had wanted to say, 'the two men who actually asked me to marry them weren't the ones I loved. I remember thinking at the time: "Dear God, I'm not settling for him! There must be better things in store for me".' She didn't say it though. She'd been patronized by Emma, in one way or another, for long enough.

She poked the fire. No pictures in it. Not for her at any rate. Perhaps fate *didn't* hold anything better in store. A jolly good job one couldn't know. Otherwise there'd be queues of people lining up to jump off high buildings; the people whose lives were rotten from start to finish—there were lives like that.

She couldn't complain; she had sufficient money, friends, a good brain. Love wasn't everything. Funny though, it was always people who'd had lots of it who came to that conclusion. Perhaps she was too discriminating, perhaps she aimed too high. Of course, she'd been spoiled—Dennis. But some woman *had* married Dennis, someone had achieved it. Oh, to be like Emma, requiring only the right sort of atmosphere to fall in love with any appropriate candidate. David said Emma was unhappy, but being unhappy was at least some sort of an emotional reaction. And, perhaps, if you didn't keep in practice, your ability to love became atrophied. Once or twice, she'd been misled; if it hadn't been for Dennis and the memory of how she'd felt *then*, she might have believed herself to be in love.

Why had he left her? Because she hadn't played the game by the rules, kept some part of her unattainable, but instead had given herself totally and generously? Whatever the reason, his conduct had left her numbed. There was a limit to the number of knocks you could be expected to take. At fourteen, worshipping the ground Robert Sainter walked on, believing him to be faultless, until Emma rudely snatched the wool away from her eyes. At seventeen, waiting on the library steps, waiting for a small, fair-haired boy, unaware until afterwards that at that very moment the small, fair-haired boy had been whirling Emma round an ice-rink. Then Dennis. In the books, these were merely object lessons one had to learn before things turned out happily ever after. The books were, perforce, neater than life.

Pinkerton, sleeping, whimpered. A dream. What sort of dreams was David, her fellow-sufferer, experiencing? The sort that blighted the whole of the morning after? She hoped not. Funny, it didn't seem like an intrusion that he should be sleeping upstairs; it seemed perfectly natural. As if all her labours to convert this house from the decaying shell it had been into a pleasant place in which to live had been so that someone else could sleep upstairs.

She wondered whether this would bring things to a head between Emma and David. Or would he be fool enough to forgive and forget? Probably. It had been obvious right from the start of their association which way the wind was blowing and if he couldn't see it then, perhaps he never would. That had been a case of affection on the rebound, if ever there was one. She remembered Emma, on the phone to him : 'Sorry, love, I can't make it tonight. We're rehearsing. Could you pop round to the flat, collect my library books and take them back, they're due today? Oh, and if you're passing the dry-cleaner's, there's my coat—'; then tarting herself up to go on the town with some man who'd said she had eyes like Elizabeth Taylor. Perhaps there *were* people fated forever to turn the other cheek and gain nothing by doing so.

Of course, Emma was a beautiful woman. And beautiful women were allowed to behave in a fashion that was forbidden to the plain and homely. After all, people didn't regard beauty as just a fortunate accident, they tended, often erroneously, to believe that beauty must possess other virtues. Which, she supposed, must make it more difficult for Emma—never knowing whether or not she was loved merely because she had eyes like Elizabeth Taylor. At least the men who'd professed to love her, Geraldine, had not been blinded by perfection of countenance.

Three o'clock. The fire was going out. Back to bed. It was very unhealthy anyway, to sit here rehashing past sadnesses. She went over to the bookcase and took out *Middle-*

march. This was an ideal time to start on all those erudite books one had put off reading for years.

David snored on. His door was ajar. In the glow from the landing light she could see that he slept in the same back-to-the-womb position as herself, his arms folded tight round his body. Emma, she thought, you deserve every bit of the retribution that's coming your way.

Thursday

David was struggling to wake from a dream in which he seemed to be pursuing Emma across a vast railway station. Over bridges, under subways, around bookstalls and waiting-rooms he raced. She appeared to be moving slowly, but always he was several yards behind and could not induce her to turn round to him. Worst of all, there was a jostling, hostile crowd around him, seemingly bent on impeding his progress.

He opened his eyes. There was an unfamiliar face above him and a hand shaking his shoulder.

'It's ten o'clock. You look as though you've been having a rare old nocturnal battle.'

He passed a hand across his eyes as though he might eradicate the last fugitive glimmer of the nightmare. Sometime, he knew, he might be able to dismiss Emma from his waking thoughts, but nothing on earth could prevent her from invading his subconscious.

'Breakfast is almost ready.'

'How can you look so bright and fresh when you must have consumed as much as me last night?'

'I couldn't sleep. I got up early and went out, making footsteps in the virgin snow. It works wonders.'

For him, it was a perfectly organized breakfast that worked wonders. Bacon and egg appeared at the table as soon as he did, the toast was hot and the coffee was strong. Breakfast with Emma was all too often hard-boiled eggs because she'd got involved inside the paper and forgotten the timing, and the smell of frying, first thing in the morning, upset her stomach for the day. And when, silently reproachful, he went kitchenwards to make himself warm toast, there'd be a curl of smoke and a voice from behind the Court Circular: 'You'd make somebody a lovely wife.' Despite, or perhaps because of, her posh upbringing, she lacked basic morning etiquette to an extent that put his teeth on edge: the butter knife in the marmalade jar, the milk bottle next to the silver sugar bowl, the refusal to pretend that rising at seven-thirty was anything more than a barbaric chore. And Emma, like all beautiful people, could look ghastly when she put her mind to it. Once perhaps, in the early days, there'd have been an almighty, comprehensive row, resulting in clear air: now, they had learnt to skirt round the edges of possible tempest, knowing that there were tactics of a more subtle and enduring cruelty.

The presiding genius of this coffee pot was dressed and groomed and capable of providing intelligent comment as well as exuding a welcome breath of early-morning freshness. He could just imagine suggesting a dawn walk over snowy fields to Emma. The response would be a heave of covers and a slim hand groping for the on-switch of the electric blanket.

'There's something about a proper, civilized breakfast with jam spoons in jam dishes which satisfies my bourgeois instincts, or so Emma tells me—bourgeois instincts, I mean.'

'Don't forget I'm entertaining. If this were a permanent arrangement, you'd probably get a snatched drink and a piece of blackened toast at the kitchen table. I expect the novelty of showing off one's culinary prowess soon wears off.'

He suspected that this was a piece of false modesty, part of her policy of non-involvement in his marital misadventures, because, when inquiring about last night's neglected washing-up and offering to hold a tea-towel, he was assured with an amused smile that all that was out of the way hours ago. Perhaps such orderly perfection could eventually wear upon the nerves, but oh, how he'd welcome it until then.

'What's our next move?' Why did there always have to be a next move?'

'We dig.'

'We dig?'

'Till we gently perspire, as we used to recite at school. Just to the end of the lane. The council should have cleared the main road by now. Our neighbouring farmer and his sons will be assisting. I visited them while I was out and borrowed you a pair of boots. They *should* fit. The farmer's sons are titanic.'

Shod in size fourteen rubber boots and equipped with a spade, he stepped outside into a muted world, a picture-postcard scene: white everywhere, till it hurt the eye. Impossible for him to resist scooping up a handful of snow just to feel it bite his fingers with its pristine coldness. 'I've never quite grown out of snow.'

'Nor have I. I have to restrain myself from snapping off icicles and putting them between my teeth, just as we used to do when we were children.'

She was wearing pants and an anorak with a blue woollen scarf knotted around her throat. They were the sort of athletic clothes that suited her well, flattered her boyish figure without in any way detracting from her femininity.

She drove her spade down into the snow. 'Heavens! It's deeper than I thought. Mr Dunn and party are working from the other end, so we should meet half-way down the lane. Shall we commence? We'll have to persuade ourselves that there really is something divine about manual labour.'

Stooping, shovelling, straightening up and throwing

99

spadefuls of snow to the side of the road, they had no breath left for conversation. Atrophied muscles protested at being called back into action; massaging his aching back and wiping his forehead with the back of his sleeve, he didn't even have the mental energy to spare for thinking. His whole concentration was fixed ahead of him, to the three men, making the same motions as himself and gradually drawing closer. It seemed that his world was safely bounded with white and ended at the pale turquoise line of the horizon. Anything beyond that was not his concern.

It took three-quarters of an hour before they clinked spades with the opposite working party. He'd been moving blindly, like an automaton; it was only when he felt steel meet steel that he looked up into a brown, grinning face whose owner said : 'Take it easy. I need both feet.'

Someone produced a Thermos of cocoa and they stood in a circle, steaming like dogs, each one trying to coax life back into his hands and filling the razor-cold air with shafts of white breath. He looked at the three big men beside him : calloused hands, rough features, placid faces. This was just one more encounter with the elements they wooed every day of their lives. Probably their wives didn't run off with other men, but if they did, it would be of less importance to them than it was to him; they had bigger, more basic problems to contend with : sowing and reaping and protecting their labours against the vagaries of nature. Perhaps the simple life was the answer.

Then the hero from the garage appeared, looking dispassionately under the bonnet of the car which was so thickly covered with snow that it might have been iced and said, 'Do you know anything about cars?'

Humbly, he explained the circumstances. The garage man obviously had no time for extenuating circumstances. 'Might be ready by late this afternoon. That's if we've got the parts.' Back to the towing wagon he trudged, giving audible voice about fools with big posh cars who weren't fit to be in charge of tricycles.

'It looks as though you're stuck with me until tea-time.'

She peeled off her sodden woollen gloves. 'Well, we'll just have to make the best of it, won't we? I'll drive into town. You can phone and we'll have lunch while we're there.'

If she was as annoyed about it as he expected her to be, then she had the good grace and accomplishment to conceal it. Worse for her than for him and Emma really, drawn unwillingly, by virtue of an unfortunate letter, into what should have been a private morass.

In the car she lit a well-earned cigarette and said, too casually, 'What will you do?'

That was a decision he intended to postpone until the eleventh hour. The idea of deliberately rehearsing a flaming row for her home-coming seemed appalling and somehow absurd. 'The trouble is, I'm only equipped for spur-of-the-moment quarrels. It would have been different if I could have tackled her immediately. But having had all this time to brood—how can I say "Your father's dying" and then in the next breath, "You adulterous slut"?'

'You really *do* love her, don't you?'

There was something about the implication of amusement in her tone that enraged him. 'You think of me as a buffoon, don't you? A deceived husband who hasn't even the guts to act in the conventional manner. I should knock her from here to kingdom come before turning her out of the house, shouldn't I? That's the accepted, manly code of behaviour. Advocated by all those men who are busy bedding their secretaries at every available opportunity. Not that I didn't try that once myself, just as an attempt to provoke her into some sort of reaction. I couldn't even go through with that when it came to the point. I kept imagining her face, aloof and mocking, like it is when she's getting the best of an argument just by keeping silent, or scared and waif-like, the way it is when she's blown up some triviality into a cosmic disaster. I never thought that casual adultery would demand some special talent. Apparently it does.'

He cleared his throat and rubbed his nose. Outbursts were foreign to his nature.

'Aren't you assuming a lot? I'm sorry. It's my fault for prying. But I think it would be better to suspend judgment until after you've heard her explanation.'

Her determination to remain neutral was almost funny. She surely couldn't be so naïve as to believe he was unaware of the probable existence of a lover? Until now though, that lover had been probable, therefore possible to endure. Upon tackling Emma, begging her to deny it, phantoms would become realities. She no longer had sufficient concern for him to spare him that final humiliation.

In the bar of the Unicorn, different from the Bell only in that horse brasses were substituted for pewter tankards, Geraldine drank ginger wine and looked across to the booth where David was telephoning for news, attempting to interpret from the set of his shoulders, the movement of his free hand, what sort of news it was.

He replaced the receiver, opened the door and came over to her. His face was expressionless. 'Operators seem to get more obtuse by the minute,' he said. He picked up his drink. 'I won't have to tell Emma her father's dying after all.' He squirted soda into his glass with a fierce precision. 'He regained consciousness at eight o'clock this morning and asked for Emma. He died at eleven.'

'God, I thought you were unconscious,' Patrick said, having called Emma's name three times to no avail before finally resorting to shaking her awake. 'You were sleeping like the dead. I was starting to panic.'

'People have been known to drop dead in the most embarrassing circumstances. What would you have done?'

'Packed very rapidly and told them downstairs to deal with the dead woman in my bed as circumspectly as possible.'

'Thanks. Funny, but last night I quite liked you.' She yawned and shuddered.

'Are you cold?'

'No. Not cold. Trying to get rid of a dream, a most unpleasant dream.'

'About what?' he said politely, but intent upon his ablutions.

'Always the same type of dream. I'm lost somewhere, no, worse than lost, abandoned. Ignored and abandoned by people who love me. When I was a kid, it was always my father—he'd fail to recognize me, or arrange to meet me then not turn up. And always it leaves me with a dreadful feeling, I call it my foreboding feeling, an acute apprehension, as though my heart was being squeezed.'

'Come along, abandoned Emma,' he said, 'have a nice hot bath and a cool shower and get your circulation going. You've got yourself into a morbid state of mind. It must be the weather.'

'The weather nothing,' she said, reluctantly climbing out of the rumpled bed. 'My foreboding feelings are almost always proved to be correct.'

'*Almost* always? Like those stories one hears about people who are prevented from catching planes which subsequently crash. Nobody mentions the scores of times they miss planes which don't crash.'

'You can mock,' she said. 'But there's usually something in it.'

'I'm sure you'd be a bombshell in a booth on the end of some pier. Failing that, let's forget about your forebodings. After all, what *could* happen?'

'Discovery—for one thing.'

'Discovery?' he said sharply. 'I've taken all possible precautions. Haven't you?'

'Of course. We certainly don't take any unnecessary risks, do we?' She could *kill* him for that look of fear which crossed his face whenever the topic of being found out was touched upon. Didn't he realize how humiliated it made her feel?

'You know very well we daren't take undue risks.' He turned to her with that now-Emma-you-know-we-must-be-sensible expression. 'It's only by *not* taking risks that we can keep this going.'

'Forget it,' she said. 'You're right. It must be the weather. Hot coffee will probably put me right.'

She lay in the bath, watching his expression change back to its normal aspect of easy-going, good nature, as he accepted at face-value her admission that she'd been unnecessarily gloomy. Would there ever be complete closeness, or would limited understanding always continue to come between them at the moment of truth? She began to soap herself with gusto. There was no reason for discontent; after all, if this didn't exist, limited though it was, she'd be sitting at home dreaming about it.

'Can you manage without me for an hour? Do some shopping, or something?' he said, as they sat down to breakfast.

'Why? Have you someone else to fit in?'

'Yes. Someone short, fat and fifty-five, if he's a day. I *am* supposed to be here on business, so I'd better make some token gesture. The chap in question is probably envisaging a five-course luncheon; he'll just have to be satisfied with a cup of coffee in the Kardomah and a lot of morale-boosting. You'll be all right Emma? I *could* put it off, if you'd rather.'

She poured his coffee. Funny, all the knowledge you assimilated then forgot: whether someone drank tea or coffee, took sugar or didn't take sugar; you looked back and found it astonishing that once you'd known someone's every involuntary gesture and now you couldn't even remember his name. 'Of course I'll be all right. You have a habit of treating me as though I'd just graduated from eating rusks. I'm a big, grown-up person and quite capable of occupying myself for an hour or two. Here, have some more toast. Get your strength back.' Playing at being married, it was all the sweeter for being pretence.

And perhaps it was a good thing for them to be separated for a short time. It gave her the opportunity to relax and recoup her energies to be again the sort of Emma he wanted.

'I'll be off then.' He put down his cup, folded his napkin and was on his feet in an instant. Always she had the feeling of being two paces behind him, in every respect. 'Get it over with. Just about an hour. I'd take you along, but this man happens to know—be acquainted with the real state of affairs.' He bent to kiss her, patting her shoulder. 'Have a nice walk. Blow away the cobwebs.'

She was left among the toast crumbs. So Beryl had been here. Oh, not to this hotel. He was too careful to make that sort of mistake. But here, to this town and district. And she, Emma, had believed it was theirs, exclusively. Beryl. She who must not be allowed to suffer.

'Has the gentleman finished?'

She looked up at the waiter with hate in her eyes, hate for all men who had the power to hurt. 'Yes, he's finished.'

She went back upstairs and put on her coat and her boots. She'd take his advice. Instead of sitting beside a fire in the lounge, hunched and brooding, she'd do something constructive, go for a walk, drift round the shops, gazing at all those beautiful objects people purchased believing them to enrich their lives. 'When I'm really down,' the woman who lived next door said, 'I buy something. It always does the trick.' The woman next door was often to be heard singing as she went about the housework. Was happiness something that could be learned? Perhaps it was all to do with one's genes, Emma thought, handing her key to the porter. And fifty per cent of her genes being of a melancholy disposition, what could you expect?

She walked aimlessly, ignorant of direction, pushed around, jostled, bumped with shopping baskets. She still had that tight, fluttery feeling in her chest. Could it be David? But David wasn't the accident-prone type. She'd ring him now from a call-box, but she knew he disliked being interrupted at the office and anyway that ultra-efficient secretary with a voice like iron-filings saying, 'I'm afraid Mr Campion is engaged at the moment. Can I help you?' gave her a pain in the neck. Tonight she'd ring him and say, 'You are OK? I had the most awful feeling.' And he'd say, 'Of course I'm OK. You won't be collecting the insurance money just yet,' if he was in one of his hearty moods. He had always thought that his heartiness was infectious; actually it grated on her nerves. And he was always in the right. How could you live with someone who was permanently in the right about everything? My husband doesn't understand me, she thought, turning in through the plate-glass doors of a department store. And in my case, it's no cliché, it's true. He's totally incapable of understanding the nuances of my mood. Emma's in a bad temper, he thinks. And that's as far as it goes. When all else fails, he'll try bribery: a holiday, new clothes, a washing machine. As if those things could make any difference. I like him so much though, that's the hell of it. I'm not certain I really *like* Patrick; sometimes, in his eyes, there's an evasive look, as though he's not to be trusted. You could trust David with your life. Not just me. Anybody. He loves me. I know he does. If only he'd say it occasionally. Sometimes I ask him and he smiles and says, 'I must do, mustn't I? Or I wouldn't put up with you.' I am **so** *sick* of people humouring me.

She stopped in the men's department. She'd buy him something. Patrick, not David. She'd never bought him anything before. The world of Christmas cards and anniversaries was not for them. There was no way of explaining gifts to one's lawful partner. But this time she'd take the chance. A tie. He could always say he'd bought it himself. Luckily he wasn't one of those men who are dressed exclusively by their wives.

'Silk,' she said to the assistant who immediately looked more interested. To match his eyes. What colour *were* his eyes? The colour of stones that have been washed by the sea for an eternity. Eyes which reflected back one's own image. She settled for a blue one. Very pretty and very expensive. From me to you, with love. Objects had no substance, but nevertheless they could serve as reminders. Perhaps every time he knots this tie, she thought, he'll think of me. Perhaps.

Package in her hand, she wandered on, into the furs. Rich, middle-aged women, wrapping themselves with sable and sealskin, well- corsetted and sleek, but every expensively-powdered face a museum.

'Can I help you madam?'

She allowed herself to be helped. Into a coat of white fox. She surveyed herself in a full-length mirror. The assistant cooed. She looked beautiful madam. She did, and she did not yet need white fox fur. She took it off and handed it back. But the time would come when she'd need it. She'd be another of these women, acquiring fur coats and gold watches and crocodile shoes like consolation prizes, while their husbands eyed young, un-made up faces and smooth, unknotted legs with yearning. When you were thirty and beautiful, you could have affairs, fall in love, to assuage your boredom. The chances of doing it became more remote with each passing year. What then? Did you have to turn into a magpie, or go mad, or resign yourself? These faces were not resigned, they were unloved and bitter. Emma beat a hasty retreat into the kitchenware where the clientele looked less likely to have the time or the money to be bored.

Thank God at least she had her drawing. Without that, she'd be nothing. A nothing, labelled with a name and a status, filed in somebody's statistics as 'Campion, Emma Julia, female, thirty, married, no distinguishing marks.' It was only when she was intent on her drawing that life became uncomplicated, that she felt she was justifying her existence. But it wasn't enough. She wanted—what? A guarantee of periodic excitement; to know that she was desired; to be convinced that she was irreplaceable. Which?

She walked out of the shop and straight into Patrick.

'Hello,' he said. He'd turned a faint shade of green. 'This is a coincidence.'

The small, bespectacled man behind him looked away politely and studied the passers-by.

'Fancy seeing you,' Emma said.

'I'm here on business. Just for a couple of days. Let me see—it must be what, two years, since we met.' His colour was returning as he gained confidence. 'At the Fergusons' party, wasn't it? What brings you here?'

'Oh, just staying with friends.' Every word cracked in the frosty air.

'Alec Mackay, let me introduce you to Emma Campion.'

Alec Mackay shook hands and inquired how long she

was staying. He wore thick-lensed glasses like the bottom of bottles; you couldn't tell what sort of assessment was being made behind them.

They stood, blocking the exit, searching for suitable words of dismissal. Alec Mackay glanced, not discreetly enough, at his watch.

'We were just going in here for coffee,' Patrick said. 'Would you like to join us, or are you in a hurry, other things to do?'

For a moment she wanted to accept his invitation, just to see him change colour again. 'I'm sorry but I really don't have the time.'

'No? Oh well. Hope to see you again soon, back in civilization. No offence Alec. It's just that the local dialect is entirely beyond me.'

They shook hands and parted from each other. She heard him talking rapidly about something else as he ushered the Mackay man through the door.

Her knees were trembling. Nothing to what his must be doing, she thought. Well, one thing was certain, she'd be able to tell him triumphantly that her foreboding hadn't been a false alarm after all. How frightened he'd appeared to be. She'd have been less alarmed in the same circumstances, but then she cared less about what she had to lose. Poor Patrick. It would be easy to hate him, but you couldn't hate someone merely because his instinct of self-preservation was paramount to all other considerations.

Afterwards, he was all apologies, but at the same time rather proud that he'd carried it off so well. 'Alec said, "Why do you always know all the attractive women?"'

'And then I suppose you had a typically coarse masculine conversation.'

'Emma,' he said reproachfully. 'You know very well I'd do no such thing.'

'So you say.'

'So I mean. You're too dear to me for me to indulge in that sort of thing.'

And it was easier to accept his word for it and take his hand, than to quarrel. But the tie remained in her suitcase, to take home for David. Now, it would have been embarrassing for her to admit she'd bought him a present as a token of their special understanding.

'I suppose Emma's mother has taken it pretty badly,' Geraldine said, breaking a silence that had lasted a full five minutes.

'She's under sedation, they said. Heavier sedation than usual, I suppose they meant.'

'When will the funeral be?'

'Monday.'

'So she'll be—'

'Yes, Emma will be back anyway.'

They turned their attention to the menu. Things should *not* be continuing as normal. Dismay should have diminished appetite. Both felt guilty at being ravenously hungry.

'What do you suppose roast duckling Elsinore might be?'

'I *know*. It is a bit, isn't it?' Geraldine said. 'It's to remind people that we're just legitimately within the county boundary of Shakespeareland. But the food's better than the trade description, I assure you.'

David looked over the top of his menu. 'Were you by any chance present at that terrible production of *A Midsummer Night's Dream* when Emma played Hermia? Hernia, she used to say.'

'I was indeed. Ghastly, wasn't it? All those fat-legged fairies fluting around.'

'She said it was something to do with having a balanced

repertoire: one week *Hedda Gabler*, the next *Autumn Crocus*. So the cast felt justified in putting their heart and soul into the one and camping up the other. Though I don't think Emma was ever dedicated to the footlights anyway.'

'It was the life she liked, not the prospect of fame: all those lavish endearments and never-ending parties and brittle theatrical wit. An actual career would have meant, for Emma, having to admit to a degree of enthusiasm she found abhorrent.'

Geraldine remembered that day when Emma had decided that there just wasn't room in the world for another Michelangelo so she'd see what the world of dramatic art had to offer instead. 'Well, in actual fact, I'll be painting scenery to start off with,' she'd said. 'But who knows how I may end up?'

'The back legs of the horse? Winding down the curtain and brewing up the tea? You'll have to take care you don't develop great biceps or you'll never make Camille.'

But Emma had merely put out her tongue and continued to sort out the items that would transform her image from artistic to theatrical.

'You're right about that,' David said. 'It was because she wasn't all actressy and superlatives that I was attracted to her in the first place. I thought she was one of those women who just fill in time with a career while they're waiting for the man to come along.'

'Not one of the ones who continue to pursue a career because the man hasn't come along?'

The implication *had* been a bit strong. He looked at her raised eyebrows. 'I didn't mean that. There must have been, be—' clumsily changing tense, 'plenty of men coming along for you.'

'Don't be trite,' she said, her tone surprisingly sharp, 'it doesn't suit you.'

Attempting to repair his blunders, he blundered on: 'Emma once told me that you were practically engaged to be married when—'

'When he took off for America? That's right. I was let down as they say in the back pages of women's magazines.' She made transverse lines with her fork across her ravioli. 'Past history. The usual sad story and of absolutely no interest to anyone but me.'

'That's the trouble, isn't it? No one's ever interested. Not even one's nearest and dearest. We can surround ourselves with husbands and wives and families, but when it all boils down it's easier to unburden to a stranger in a train.'

'You're right, but there's nothing much we can do about it, is there? It's the reason why good advice is rarely followed. We're unable to identify with one another.'

She stared down into her plate. A young Chinese, waiting for his lover to cross a bridge. Prepared to die for her. Just a story on a plate.

'Why did it break up?'

'Ask him,' she said. 'He's now somewhere in Sussex, I believe, doubtless raising roses and children. He might have a bit of difficulty in placing my name though. Why does any relationship break up? Because people can rarely love in direct ratio. Ask Emma even. She told me I'd frightened him off with my intensity. And Emma was always better qualified on that particular subject than me.'

Oh that Oxford summer. All the days had been hot days. Days when she had to keep pinching herself to make sure she wasn't just dreaming of delight. Her first lover. Sequestered Sunday afternoons, making love between the stripes of sunlight that flooded his room, ecstatic and amazed that God could be so good as to allow him to return her love. Then the airport and the letters, then no more letters and wild hopes: a one-day postal strike, a devilish liaison between the postman and the porter's lodge, then the Easter vacation and the end of self-deception. Daffodils in church and Christ usurping her position on the cross. All those cigarettes and a postcard of the Uffizi from Emma. Trying to cry quietly because the walls were paper-thin.

'I tried to gas myself,' she said. 'But it takes a lot of guts to gas yourself. I've never told anybody about that before.'

She watched the expressions flitting across his face. 'I should imagine the correct reaction would be one of politely restrained disbelief,' she said. 'But feel free.'

He looked at her curiously. It was Emma he could imagine crouched by the hearth, feeding shillings into the gas meter. Then he realized that such action demanded a character of no compromise and it was obvious that this woman possessed it; Emma, on the other hand, would grab at any life-saver, be it alcohol or nicotine, music or love, believing it to lead to happiness or at least oblivion.

'I'm sorry,' he said. 'I'm sorry that you could ever have been so disillusioned with yourself that you could contemplate doing such a thing.'

'Disillusioned with myself? Yes, I suppose you're right. I'd never had much faith in my lovableness. Him behaving in that way intensified my belief that no one wanted what I could offer. Afterwards, I vowed, I swore, I would never allow myself to be put into a position of such vulnerability again.'

She placed her knife and fork together. 'Forgive me. I've no business to be adding to your miseries. What shall we have? Gâteau Juliette? Tarte aux pommes Desdemona? It can't be true!'

'I'm glad you told me. Somehow it helps to know that other people have weathered crises. I'd always thought of you as being fearsomely in control. Not at all the sort of person in whose company I could get drunk.'

'What a pity it had to take this to explode that particular myth.'

'This.' He stared right through a woman at the opposite table who began to experiment with her profile. He was definitely the kind of man to attract that sort of behaviour, the kind of man you'd make a bee-line for at a party after you'd been dazzled by the flashier ones. 'For a moment I'd forgotten about "this"—not forgotten exactly, but pushed it into a convenient subliminal recess. Isn't it possible to leave it there for a few more hours? Keep talking. Tell me about you. It's entirely due to you that I've kept my sanity this long.'

She smiled. She had a good, genuine smile, mercifully free from any trace of coquetry. Why didn't she smile more often? Perfect teeth were uncommon.

'I'd be only too delighted,' she said. 'It's every woman's dream, to receive a request for her personally edited auto-biography. But I think you'd be asleep all among your apples Desdemona before I'd been going ten minutes.' She smiled again. 'My mother always used to say that people were much nicer to each other during the war. It's a bit like that with us. Like enemies trapped together in a trench under bombardment suddenly discovering common sympathies.'

He winced at her analogy.

'Well it's true. You haven't forgotten that, by definition, we are on different sides of the metaphorical fence?'

He didn't tell her that no fence existed for him. How very much simpler it would be if it did.

Like two somnambulists, Patrick and Emma walked along a parallel infinity of deserted pier. Viewed from a distance, they might have been one figure, so harmoniously did their rhythms blend. Gazing across a Sahara of grey

sand to a sea the colour of slate, it seemed incredible that
in a couple of months the place would be pulsing with
humanity and candyfloss and the reiterated nostalgia of fair-
ground tunes. Today the only sound to rend the lowering
sky was the scream of seagulls, swerving low and inland to
scavenge humanity's debris. Lowering. He liked that word.
A phrase from the long stupor of afternoon Shakespeare
periods at school came into his mind and he said it aloud:
'And all the clouds that lour'd upon our house in the deep
bosom of the ocean buried.'

'I liked that too. Oh the dramatic possibilities of being
cast as an offstage voice: And fall thy edgeless sword:
Despair, and die! When the film came out, we were
marched through the streets in an endless navy-blue crocodile to be edified at the Trocadero Cinema. They'd wondered whether perhaps it might be too gory for our tender
young sensibilities. They needn't have worried. We sat
entranced throughout, avidly waiting for the reappearance
of a certain courtier who must have had the shortest
doublet and the tightest pair of hose in the entire history of
film production.'

'A real-life equivalent of the glossy tomes of art studies
you doubtless pored over in the school library?'

'Yes. All we'd discovered from those was that if the
ancient Greeks were anything to go by, everyone seemed to
be making a great fuss about a very little.'

How sweet she must have been. How sweet all little girls
were. He supposed that was the reason she'd wanted to
re-create that childhood visit, to prove that once, she had
been young and incorrupt.

'Look!' She gestured to a faint shape on the horizon that
might be mirage or might be land. 'Is it Ireland?'

'Not unless we're in the middle of a seismographic upheaval and the seas are running dry. It could be Anglesey.'

She was a mine of esoteric information, but there were whole areas of knowledge about which she was surprisingly ignorant. As she described it : 'I've never been able to grasp the fact that you don't step off the globe at the North Pole and on to it again at the South. I'm just a natural flat-earther.'

Well, it tied in very well with her policy of non-question-ing acceptance. This excursion to a desolate, out-of-season, seaside town had been to indulge her whim. For him, it meant a welcome lethargic interlude sandwiched between the frenetic days of his real existence, but for her, he felt, it represented the type of languorous inactivity that was closest to her essential self.

Having surveyed the panorama from the end of the pier : a sleeping vastness of grey upon grey—the non-scene, as painstakingly depicted by a zealous townswoman, only to be hung in that part of the gallery where no one ever pauses—and plunged forcibly into unwelcome wakefulness by a blast of ozone that carried with it the odour of a thousand decaying shellfish, they turned their steps town-wards.

An ancient poster, advertising the last production of the summer season repertory theatre, caught Emma's eye. 'God, that brings back memories.'

'Oh, I forgot. You had a phase of the Ellen Terrys, didn't you?'

'It was rather more than a phase,' she said with dignity. 'It was nearly three years.'

'What happened? Did you never find the right casting-couch that would have opened up the West End to you?'

Most of the time she liked his easy, flippant manner. She'd always detested those people labelled as sincere. There were some areas, however, in which glibness was not the right reaction. Laugh at other people, she thought, but please don't laugh at me.

'The casting-couch is largely a myth. I would never have made the West End in a million years. I just played a host of dim ingenues in a dim fashion in two not-outstanding repertory theatres.' And I adored every minute of it: the tears and the tantrums, the squalid digs where they asked you which was your bath night, the great mugs of tea and the scrambled egg sandwiches which seemed to be my whole diet, with the odd meat pie thrown in, for three years. 'I was a lousy actress, but I adored it.' Her face shone, her memory selecting the happier images from the whole. 'There was a kind of un-monotonous continuity about it that suited me.' Life would never again be so highly-coloured, tightly-constructed and gay.

'It means a lot to you, doesn't it, continuity?'

'The lack of it frightens me. No, more than that, it makes me despair.' She gathered in the pier, the Marine Drive, the shuttered café and the swimming baths with a sweep of her arm. 'In a hundred years, if this still exists, someone will stand here, just on this spot, and they won't know that one February morning Patrick and Emma, who loved each other, stood here too. That, I can come to terms with. What bothers me is that in ten or twenty years *we'll* still be alive and all that's passed between us will have dwindled away to nothing.'

He took her hand, smoothing the skin over the knuckles as though he might smooth the lines of misgiving from her forehead. 'I don't think either of us is that callous, are we?'

'It's nothing to do with being callous. It's inevitable. The wonder of us will be reduced to a few occasions of sexual pleasure. "What was her name? Emma. That's it. We had some nights together." That's all it will be.'

He'd thought of her as a day-to-day creature, but he

117

couldn't believe that any woman could enter a relationship completely devoid of hope. 'Emma, you can't look at life like that. You must have loved other men and that love, in some way, will have enriched your life.'

'Men like you always talk about love as though it were something that could be parcelled up and set aside for appropriate occasions.'

'Men like me?'

'Yes, men like you. The only sort women like me are attracted to. And anyway, contrary to popular supposition, I have loved only one other man. And the outcome of that certainly did nothing to enrich my life.'

'Always analysing, aren't you?' he said. 'Don't search and probe. Just be. Accept that we make each other happy. Don't ask too much.'

He put an arm round her shoulders. She looked up into his face for a clue, some clue. How can I be sure that what I feel for this face, this body, is love? she thought. When I'm coming to meet him, or going away from him, I'm so unsure. Then, when a week passes without hearing from him, I'm demented. I smoke and listen to music and read his few letters over and over again, trying to detect notes of falsity in them. And when we're together, I seem to go into some sort of rapturous trance from which it's impossible to analyse my feelings at all.

They began the long walk back to where he'd parked the car. Past a pink-washed grand hotel, behind whose double-glazing, conference delegates doodled round the edges of their notes and yawned at each other over dull expanses of green baize. Past a tidy row of private hotels where old ladies of independent means adjusted crocheted shawls round their shoulders while they crocheted more shawls to adjust round their shoulders. Past shops whose boarded windows concealed everything cheap, garish and nasty that could make the holiday go with a swing. Past terraced gardens and green park benches where other, less favoured, illicit lovers would perform their rituals as soon as darkness fell.

Her hand lay cold, ungloved in his. Fragile, child-size fingers, fashioned for nothing more strenuous than love or wielding a delicate pencil. How totally defenceless she appeared to be. Beryl was made of sturdier stuff, a reassuring combination of common-sense and vigour, the sort of woman who'd prove the biologists correct by staying alive under conditions that would finish a man hours earlier; during his absences from Beryl, he was never plagued by worries of her not being able to cope, in the way that he visualized Emma walking a tightrope above a chasm of calamity.

The railway station buffet provided scalding, welcome tea which left layers of yellow around the insides of their cups as its level diminished.

'It's years since I had this. It's another pervasive memory of my itinerant repertory days : cross-country journeys, fortified with railway tea and five Woodbines at the station buffet. Always convinced that, bound for Birmingham, I'd end up in Edinburgh. That was the time of the man who never took me to the West End.' Hyacinth eyes reading portents in the tea-leaves. Old love. Impossible to describe without resorting to over-sentimentality. 'He's quite famous now. I see his face on posters or the television and blush to remember all the unguarded things I said. And I know that those things I said washed over him without leaving a trace.'

'Was it so terrible?'

'Its outcome was catastrophic. Funny, I'd never believed that rubbish about seeing someone across a room and being spellbound. But that's how it was. And after I'd ceased to love him, I was appalled that my judgment could be so treacherous. I daresay I was ready to be in love and he was the likeliest candidate around. It wasn't even that he was outstandingly good-looking. That, I could have understood. I was at the age when looks can go a long way towards clouding one's view.'

'It's the tone of a voice, a glimpse of a profile, something tiny and fugitive which seems to recall an obscure memory, as though you've met each other somewhere before.' He broke off as a cleaner began to poke around their feet with a malodorous mop. 'Oh God. Let's get out.'

Obediently she followed him to the door and stood, inhaling deep breaths of sharp sea air while he went to the Gents. If only she could discuss things with him, take apart their relationship to see whether, beneath the gloss of attraction and adventure, there was something that made it different from other people's squalid affairs. But he refused to be pinned down, always laughing and moving on when she began to touch upon fundamentals.

He reappeared from white tiles and Gothic lettering; slim, muscular body negotiating the curving steps two at a time, dark curls damp and disordered, cigarette drooping from his lower lip, giving him the look of a B film tough. She loved him, there was no question about it. She wanted to tell him all about that other man she'd loved, wanted him to listen, to absolve her and to reassure her that his love for her was not like that, not like that at all.

A junior girl, lunching with her parents in the Unicorn, saw Geraldine and nudged her mother.

'Oh dear, that means a certain amount of giggling speculation tomorrow morning,' Geraldine said, smiling coolly over to the corner table.

'Why?'

'That little fair-haired girl in the corner is one of my pupils.'

'And will she report back to her classmates?'

'Indubitably. The little ones spend the greater part of their time fantasizing about our private lives.'

'And are they accurate?'

'They're astute, I don't know about accurate. In a relatively small place like this they don't miss much and they've only to see you exchange a greeting with someone of the male sex for them to blow it up into a great romance. The fact that they consider I am over the age limit to indulge legitimately in great romances will only add to the interest.'

'You're the same age as Emma, aren't you?'

'Yes. But from the viewpoint of their tender eyes thirty might just as well be fifty.'

'It sounds perfectly dreadful.'

'No. It's not dreadful. I made a big decision—to go into teaching—and I can't say that I've really regretted it. You move within a tight, tidy framework and, as Emma will doubtless have told you, I tend to be obsessively neat.'

Actually Emma's description, years ago, had been 'typical thin, angular, chain-smoking intellectual: Lady Margaret Hall, black jumpers and *Beowulf*, that sort of thing'—but then Emma had always tended towards oversimplification.

'What made you decide to leave Oxford?' he asked her. 'I understood you were researching into something very erudite.'

'I had to leave Oxford,' she said. 'Make a break. Every street and landmark was a torture to me; that they could look the same as ever, even though they'd witnessed my misery. I liked Oxford, I was cocooned, concentrating solely on those things I found congenial, but if I hadn't left, I would have had a breakdown. One tends not to believe people who advise a complete change of environment as a cure, but it *does* work—believe me.'

'Is that what you'd advise me to do?'

She thought he was being facetious, but his expression was perfectly serious. 'Your circumstances are different. You can't drop everything and move on as I did. I had nobody but me to think about.'

'Perhaps I'd be doing her a service if I did go.'

'A service?' Her eyebrows were two question-marks again. 'Don't you *know* Emma by now? She's got to have somebody. She'd simply crack up on her own. She hasn't the —I don't know—the stamina to exist as a self-sufficient unit.'

It had always been the same with Emma: she could tell him a thing or two: the way she fastened on to somebody, anybody. Once, when they were at school, some friend had jilted her, so she'd allowed a middle-aged roué she'd met at her father's firm's dinner dance to take her out to tea. And that's all it was: tea, she'd insisted sullenly when all was discovered and the headmistress had telephoned her father just like 'a damned moral welfare committee,' as he'd put it. Probably it had been only tea; he was somebody and that was all Emma wanted.

'We're back on the same topic,' David said. 'Apparently there's no escape from it. Shall we go?'

Outside, she began to walk towards the car, but he halted her. 'Is that a park over there? Would you mind a walk? Or have you done enough walking for one day? Somehow I feel better when I'm on the move.'

'No,' she said. 'I don't mind.' The whole situation was so peculiar, she thought, that they might as well do peculiar things like walking in the park with the temperature touching freezing-point.

He took her arm as they walked along the icy paths. She

felt herself to be tense; always she had been averse to physical contact unless it was physical contact between herself and a lover, but gradually they fell into a sort of rhythm, clinging to each other in order to remain upright. Once, she lost her footing and slid for a yard. He just managed to catch her in time or she'd have been flat on her face. 'You'd be safer if you held on to my hand,' he said. So she did, in the most neutral fashion possible, talking rapidly and sensibly all the time in order to take her mind off the fact.

Through the frosted trees and around the frozen lake they walked and encountered only one old man, bent on his constitutional, and a couple of vagrant dogs. No sound in the air except the crack of ice beneath their feet and sometimes their hushed voices whispering back at them from the echo chamber of a tunnel of firs.

'It's eerie,' she said. 'I wouldn't care to be here alone, even in daylight.'

'You're not the nervous type, are you? I wouldn't have thought so. Living where you do isn't exactly ideal for someone of a nervous disposition.'

'I don't mind that so much. There, I'm enclosed. There's nothing inside to harm me. But out here anything can come at you, from any direction. It's all beyond my control, like high winds or thunder and lightning.'

'How curious.' He stopped to skim a stone across the lake. It was an unsuccessful attempt. Some things you were only capable of doing in your childhood. 'Most curious. My wife has the opposite sort of fear: the dark at the top of the stairs, the nameless terror behind the clothes in the wardrobe. Yet she's at the top of her form during thunderstorms, animated by all that extra electricity flying round I daresay, and once, when we were staying in the Lake District with some friends, she went out for a walk in the woods and didn't return until after dark. Everyone was rushing round with torches and hurricane lamps, but she arrived back quite unperturbed, saying why on earth should she have been afraid.'

'Perhaps Emma is rather more elemental a creature than me.'

'If that means she blows with the prevailing wind, then you're right.' He cupped his gloved hands and blew into them. 'We're certainly getting our fair share of fresh air today. I'm not freezing you to death, am I?'

'It's supposed to be a remedy for insomnia.'

'Are you a sufferer?'

'Yes,' she said. 'And please spare me the usual explanation for my difficulty in sleeping.'

'Oh.' He grinned. 'I wasn't going to say that. Anyway—'

'Anyway what?'

'Anyway nothing.' Anyway, if that was the case, he'd been going to say, I'd be awake and staring into many a grey dawn. 'Tell me,' he said, 'what do you do with yourself here, apart from teaching the rudiments of the English language to several hundred little girls?'

She shrugged her shoulders. 'The usual things. The cinema, concerts, there's a theatre, drive, walk, knit sweaters. Just the same boring routine everybody else follows.'

'I should imagine it's a dead sort of town.'

'One place is much the same as another. Maybe some places have more opportunities for amusement, but I bet it's just as easy to be bored in South Kensington as it is to be bored here.'

'I'm sorry,' he said. 'I didn't mean to adopt that awful patronizing London tone. There's precious little excitement where I live anyway. They probably raise more hell in a village hall on a Saturday night.'

124

'Where you live can't alter the quality of your life. You wouldn't expect the rich to be bored, would you, having the power to purchase all manner of distractions? But many of them are, nevertheless. On the other hand, there are people who could occupy themselves happily on a desert island.'

'I suppose it depends on the amount of *joie de vivre* you happen to be born with,' he said.

'Or the way you manage to discipline yourself.'

They walked on, past the bowling green, the tennis courts, the children's playground. Her hand in his was now more relaxed. What a pleasant change it was to walk beside a woman who wasn't always deep in thought and silent. Perhaps it was all a question of complementary metabolic rates; he and Emma were both inclined to sink into lethargy instead of resorting to the good old remedy of action to banish the hump.

'There's one thing about all this,' he said. 'At least I'm aware that I'm at a turning point in my life. Mostly you pass that point before you realize it, like reading your horoscope two weeks late and finding out you should have taken that big chance after all.'

'You don't read horoscopes, do you?'

'Yes. Don't you?'

'I pretend not to, but actually I do. I suspect everyone does—seeking for guidance, however trivial it may be. I see what you mean about turning points though. It's both a good and a bad thing. It means you needn't look back in five years' time and think : if only I'd known, but on the other hand you haven't the excuse of ignorance to comfort you.'

He pushed a child's swing to and fro; it seemed as if fidgeting helped to release his tension.

'Perhaps we'll meet again in a year or two,' she said, 'and

prefer to forget this conversation. On the whole, inaction is the easier alternative.'

He gave the swing one final, vicious push which sent it soaring into the white sky. 'Oh no,' he said. 'There are some things which make a difference, which mean you just can't continue as before. Even between us—well, we've come to know each other better. In a year or two, we couldn't be in that sort of stupid frame of mind to prefer to forget things. We've come beyond that.'

She cleared snow from the railings. Some days, you felt prettier, lighter, altogether more well-favoured. Crazily enough, this was turning out to be one of those days.

In the writing room of the Majestic, Emma sought to appropriate a hotel pen, found it was chained to the desk, so contented herself with doodling round the edge of the blotter until Patrick came back from requesting service. Snow had forced them to remain indoors. She stared out of the window, willing the flakes to fall faster and thicker, though she knew it was pointless—he was the man to find an escape route through a polar ice cap.

He came up behind her. 'It seems to be siesta hour. Is tea such a very strange request at three-thirty in the afternoon?'

Whether it was or not, he'd get it. He was the type who got what he wanted. There were people, she'd discovered, who always got what they wanted. Something to do with their astrological pattern, or perhaps it was just the way they went about it.

'What are you doing?'

'Well, as the *Vogues* and the *Ideal Homes* and the *Amateur Gardeners* are all last year's, I'm making out a list of four-star hotels I have adultered in.'

He pursed his lips and nodded his head. '*Touché*. If I could arrange a less music-hall-joke alternative, believe me,

I would do.' Looking over her shoulder, he saw her entangled design of circles and spirals. 'Know yourself from your unconscious scribbles,' he said.

'And from your profound studies of *Reader's Digest* articles, what conclusions do you draw?'

'Oh, spirals are bad, and I'm sorry to say, circles are worse.' He lifted her hair from the back of her neck and kissed her gently on the spot that he knew would make her dissolve.

'I'm sorry Patrick. It's just that—'

'I know, I know.' He turned her round and silenced her incoherence with his lips. The reluctant waiter who had been called away from the television set during the last crucial furlong of the 3.30 arranged cups and plates on a low table with an expression of bored disapproval.

Emma put out her tongue at his retreating back. 'All the world loves a lover. Do you remember the time you kissed me in that pub full of insurance agents and travellers-in-ladies'-underwear discussing their mortgages over half-pints of bitter, and there was this thirty-second silence, then everyone began talking furiously again? People can accept public hostilities much more easily than public displays of affection.'

'Come and preside over the Crown Derby.'

They surveyed toast and sandwiches and slices of that sort of cake known at school as yellow peril which they didn't particularly want and which had been ordered solely to establish tea-time and therefore go some way towards arranging their day.

'D'you suppose humanity will be kind enough to leave us in peace?' she said. Sitting beside a coal fire, silver teapot and cake crumbs, it seemed like home, the home they could only establish briefly and in alien hotel rooms.

'And if they do leave us in peace, how shall we pass this

snowbound afternoon, dearest Emma?' Even his leer was attractive.

'Well, not in the way you're imagining, that's for certain. Beds have to be made and floors Hoovered you know and a "do not disturb" notice at three-thirty p.m. is going beyond the bounds of British decency. We could recite poetry, or write postcards home, or perhaps you have a deck of cards about your person, if you find my company insufficiently stimulating.'

'The only poems I know are about young ladies called Alice. And your company is quite sufficient in itself.' He lit cigarettes for both of them, took her hand and settled back into the cushions.

He looks tired, she thought. All those other parts of his life, the parts I can't really believe exist because they don't concern me, they make him tired. I'm supposed to realize that and act accordingly. He just hasn't the capacity to care about my troubles as well. Why is it that the men who'd be willing to hang on to my every word are never the ones I fancy?

'It's cosy here,' he said, moving her head more comfortably into the angle of his shoulder. And for perhaps twenty minutes she remained, passive, warm and comfortable, within the circle of his arm. But she was fighting a losing battle with an insistent, nagging voice which said 'All very well to sit here, indulging a fantasy that this is a permanent state of affairs, but you know very well that tomorrow it will be over and you won't know each other any better than you did before. For God's sake, let's have some honesty, even if it's unpalatable.'

'Do you believe in patterns?' she said.

'Patterns?' Though he wasn't too surprised. She was an artist when it came to the non-sequitur.

'Yes, patterns in life. Events repeating themselves, but,

worse than that, the knowledge that one is reacting to those
events in precisely the same misguided way as before. Several
years ago I spent a few days with a man in an out-of-season
seaside resort.' She watched his face. For all she could read
into his expression, she might have been looking at a profile
on a Greek vase. 'And that too was in the nature of being
an illicit week-end.'

'So?'

'So, he went away and you'll go away too, won't you?'

She'd known him long enough to recognize his small
personal signs of irritation : a certain jerky way of pulling
down his cuffs, a quick involuntary twitch of the eyebrows,
but some masochistic desire to dig and disinter drove her
on. 'It's just that I can't believe the pattern will change.'

'Presumably he—this man, whoever he was—left because
it was the time to leave, or because circumstances forced
him to leave. You can talk about patterns if you like. But
that's just life.'

How simple it was in his philosophy. Just life. Could one
acquire the talent for coming to terms, or was it an inborn
asset. 'But if I hadn't chanced to meet him and spent that
weekend with him, my life would have turned out differently.'

'I doubt it. Anyway, what's wrong with your life that this
disappearing guy managed to perpetrate?'

'There's something you don't know, Patrick. Nobody
knows, except Geraldine. And Gerry's one of those fine,
upstanding, silent-as-the-grave people when it comes to
keeping secrets. It's something I want you to know, but I'm
afraid to tell you in case your opinion of me takes a rapid
nose-dive.'

'Try me.'

'It's not a nice piece of information.'

'You turn into a werewolf every twenty-eight days? Come

to think of it, I've never met you during full-moon. You're really a fellow? You went to Casablanca and had the operation?'

She turned from him and gazed into the fire. 'I bore you, don't I, when I'm being serious?'

'Jesus Christ, Emma! Stop behaving like some coy adolescent and tell me if you want to tell me. Otherwise don't tell me and stop looking so doomy.'

So she told him. About that other man with whom she'd once shared the afternoon tea cakes and scones in a seaside hotel.

Scarborough. Cold, so cold, even in the summer. And those digs! The landlady fiddled the gas meter so that it only gave off enough heat to make trellis-work patterns on your shins. Sitting on the radiators in the theatre, risking piles, just to absorb some feeble warmth. And that time the boiler broke down! She'd gone home with her chilblains to have pleurisy in comfort. Her father had said, 'I suppose there's a certain romance to be found in squalor when one is young.' And then, 'One of your actor friends has just rung. I told him you weren't allowed out of bed. He didn't give his name—very deep, peremptory voice.' And she'd flown down the stairs, her dressing-gown open and a temperature of a hundred and two, to ring him back.

John Austin. Small, dark and destined for better things. A brilliant actor and a bit of a bastard, they'd said, when they heard he was joining them. They were right. But she'd accepted the one as she'd accepted the other. In her limited experience, the two were indivisible. 'I do have a wife, you know,' he'd told her. 'So nothing can come of it. It will all end in tears, as nanny used to say.' Humbly she'd acknowledged the information, she, who, a year before, had had half a dozen men at her beck and call, who'd left them standing under some clock or told her flat-mate to say she was unavailable, now reconciled to waiting for telephone calls that never came, outings that didn't materialize because he had to dash back to London to see important people or spend Sunday with Ruth. It was the first time she'd been in love and, despite her knowledge that he had neither the right nor the propensity to love her, she couldn't believe that life could be so perverse as to let such an expenditure of loving go to waste.

Just a year they'd had together. Scarborough. Walking along the beach. Stumbling over those hard ribs carved in the sand. His movements were controlled, agile, feline. He'd take her elbow and steer her round watery pitfalls and mounds of sea-washed sediment. Observed only by birds and molluscs and a man with a pair of binoculars in a front bedroom of the Marine Hotel, they'd explore the salt sweetness of each other's mouths. And afterwards, in his flat, they'd open tins, cook the contents on one gas ring, and in the brass bed, beneath a picture of a simpering wood nymph with draperies positioned deliberately to titillate, he'd say her name, over and over again, as if it was only she who could quench some great thirst.

She'd known he'd go, sometime he'd go. What she hadn't known was the extent of the horrors that would follow upon his departure. A railway station—the train was late, they had to struggle to converse while they waited, a sudden blinding hatred of the town that it could continue to exist after he'd left it, and, a week later, a picture-postcard of the Peter Pan statue in Kensington Gardens: 'Always, John.' Always, John. Never John.

'So you had an affair with some inconsiderate, self-obsessed get,' Patrick said. 'It happens to all of us at some time. I was fourteen when Muriel Evans threw me over for a bigger boy. I couldn't eat for a fortnight. I recovered though. We're more resilient than we like to think. What's the point of dredging it up?'

'I'm telling you about *me*. Are you afraid to know about me? Or is it just that you're not interested? Emma. All right in small doses. All right as long as she remembers the limits of her position. A mistress. Or perhaps I'm not even granted that exalted title. Perhaps I'm just the woman who's always on hand and always grateful when you fancy a sexual diversion.'

Face flushed, voice cracking. Never could display anger in a dignified fashion.

'You're just being stupid and what's worse you know you're being stupid.'

'I agree. I am stupid. Women who aren't stupid take good care to avoid this kind of mess.'

He stood up, pocketing his cigarettes and lighter. 'I'm not going to row with you Emma. I could stay at home for a row. I'm going upstairs until you've recovered from the glooms. For God's sake, leave the past alone. I don't want to *hear* about your other lovers. Do you want to hear about mine? It's exactly the same thing. Don't ruin what we have. Those other people, they're ghosts, they went away and left you for me and me for you. That's all that matters.'

But it wasn't the going away that did the harm, she thought. It was the coming back.

They made it up of course. In the usual way. There were people, she believed, who fought just so that they could make it up in bed. She'd come into the room and found him sorting through business papers. An apologetic expression, a touch of his cheek and he'd put aside his work and pulled her on to the bed. They'd worked out their aggression through the act of love. It had been a contest, each one waiting for the other to capitulate with a cry. And the first cry, as always, had been hers.

Sexual necessity, if nothing else, would continue to bind her to him. In the bathroom, she inspected her body. A mark on her neck. Until now they'd been very careful about that sort of thing. Wear a scarf. Cover it with Elastoplast. I grazed it on the bathroom cabinet. David might not even recognize it for what it was. It had been that long. However, God was good. He could have arranged it so that a scarlet A would appear on one's forehead afterwards. Must remember to phone tonight. Keep him happy. Maybe he's happy anyway. I don't contribute much to his well-being. He can invite one of his dreary, prematurely middle-aged friends around and they can discuss the match, or the mortgage, or some other equally boring subject without me looking glassy-eyed and clearing my throat. Oh David, if only you knew. Knew that I was standing here warm and glowing from love. What would you do?

'Come back.'

He lay on the bed, one arm beneath his head, magnificent and somehow pagan in his nakedness. Pan, smiling and satiated.

'What are you thinking Emma?' He caught and held her hand, entwining their fingers.

'I was thinking that you look like a tom-cat. And get some clothes on in case a chambermaid comes in to turn down the bed or something.'

'And falls upon me with lust in her eyes? She'd be wasting her time I'm afraid.' He stretched, from his fingers to his toes. 'I'm happy.'

'Why shouldn't you be? You're a typical male animal. All you require is food and drink and a plentiful supply of sex.'

'That's my Emma. You are my Emma again, aren't you?'

And, feeling a sudden pang of compassion for his natural

male incomprehension, she stroked his hair and told him she was. Perhaps it was essential that you were all things to all people. Perhaps it was too much to hope that you'd eventually find one person capable of recognizing and accepting you in all your aspects.

He got up, whistling. Into the bathroom, and through the roar of water, she could hear his baritone rendering of 'Girls were made to love and kiss' interspersed with 'Must I shave, Emma? Am I likely to be coming into close contact with anyone again today? All this love-making. It's nothing but shave, shave, shave.'

She smiled into the mirror. Needing such a little to make him happy. John was like that. A great zest for life. Mascara brush in hand, she paused. It seemed as though she needed men like that. She'd always regarded herself as wronged, but perhaps it wasn't that at all. Perhaps she was some kind of succubus. Perhaps John had fled for his life. Absent-mindedly she began to brush her eyelashes. Perhaps that was the thing that would eventually lose her Patrick. She was an emotional parasite, she knew that. Previously though, she'd regarded a parasite as a pathetic little creature. But it could be deadly too.

'Do I smell nice?' He put his arms round her neck and rubbed his face against the smooth black fall of hair and heard it crackle.

'There, I told you we generate a current between us.'

She looked at their faces, reflected next to each other. 'What beautiful babies we'd produce. Beautiful, black-haired babies. Don't worry.' He could never disguise the flicker of consternation that crossed his face whenever an oblique reference to that subject was made. 'If I am, we'll sue.'

She'd never told him that, for six years, she'd proved to be sterile. She accepted it—it was a just punishment, after all

—but she couldn't tell him. She felt inadequate enough without admitting she couldn't fulfil that supreme female function.

Two seaside hotels, two men. That other time had been so unbelievably corny: potted palms and fat men entertaining their secretaries to quiet weekends. That other time, she'd met her doom. Oh yes, it sounded very melodramatic, but it was true all the same.

A November afternoon. She'd recovered. She had David. Dear dependable David. If he said he'd be there at seven, he'd be there at seven, come fire or flood. It was good to be treated like something precious. The phone had rung and, cursing, she'd padded, dripping and pink from the bath, to answer it. 'Emma?' And uncontrollable panic even before she'd definitely placed the voice. 'I couldn't find myself in this neck of the woods and not get in touch with you. Though it's quite by chance I found you out. I bumped into Nick Thompson and he gave me your number.' Could she get the weekend off? Dearest Emma, she couldn't know how it felt to hear her voice again. She hadn't got herself married, or anything, had she? Emma?

Eighteen months. Eighteen months since she'd wandered round that rotten town, looking speculatively over the end of the pier, and for him, gay and calm, it might have been yesterday.

But whatever strength you needed to be able to say go to hell, she didn't possess it. A lie for David, and at seven o'clock she was waiting at the front door, her suitcase at her feet.

Everything about him the same: thin fingers with dark hair growing aslant to the knuckles, high-bridged, narrow nose, curved mouth, like the young Tennyson's before the beard, eyes black and sweet. 'We're old friends, aren't we Emma?' No, a thousand times no. They were old lovers with old vibrations stirring between them. Each casual touch awakened the memory of so many nights, all so different, so alike. To think of refusing to accompany him would be to reduce all those other nights to nothing.

And afterwards, after they'd booked into that hotel with her wearing a gold signet ring the wrong way round on the relevant finger and trying to remember whether he took sugar in his coffee, and he lay, a pale profile, beside her, afterwards it was over. The ghosts had been exorcised. She looked at him and saw a man with a cruel mouth and a receding hairline, a man whom she had once loved and loved no longer.

Notoriously forgetful, she could remember every detail of that other room, just as she would remember every detail of this one. An unremarkable room : everything in shades of beige, but she'd remember it. And she'd see Patrick, buttoning his shirt and saying, 'You look so pretty Emma.' Herself, painting a face behind which the real, shrinking Emma could face the world, slim and dark and wearing a blue, ribbon-trimmed slip. She saved all her best things for him. He'd have died if he could have seen the tattered old flannelette things she normally slept in.

'Well Emma. We've had our first row. And our first reconciliation.'

Our first taste of reality, she thought. Any more of it and the fragile structure we call a relationship would probably totter and crumble. I thought we might be able to tell each other everything, including those shameful things that only return to plague us sometimes during sleepless nights. I made a mistake.

'It's something of a landmark, you know,' he said. 'I thought the fact that you never quarrelled was what made me love you. Now I find I love you more because we've quarrelled.'

He stood beside her, tall, attractive, and pleased with himself. I made a mistake, she thought. He's charming and I couldn't do without him, but fundamentally he's the same as the others, a smaller man than I imagined him to be.

'It's three o'clock,' Geraldine said. 'We might as well drive home until your car's ready. The roads are better now and there's nothing much to do here unless you fancy *How the West Was Won* at the Rialto, or improving your mind with a trek round the art gallery.'

'I don't think I could even summon up the concentration for *How the West Was Won*. I'd prefer to go back—that's if you don't mind. I'm not messing things up, am I? I mean, you didn't have plans made for something else, did you?'

'No. Nothing special.' Nothing at all would have been the truthful answer, but it was too humiliating to admit the paucity of one's life to anyone else. Someone with a richer existence would have been less involved; she had to recognize a certain malicious satisfaction in witnessing other people's messes. The natural satisfaction of the unloved woman when she hears that lovers have come to grief, she told herself as she reconnoitred the car round a nasty patch of ice. Not jealousy any more. She'd grown out of that six years ago when she'd seen at first hand just what a pretty pass Emma's amorous adventures had brought her to.

'How old was he?' she said.

'Fifty-seven.' There was no need for him to ask who she meant. Whatever tangents their thoughts might pursue, they always returned, inevitably, to that one irrefutable fact.

'I think perhaps he died at the right time. I couldn't imagine him declining gracefully into chaste old-age, could you?'

'If he'd declined gracefully a long time ago, maybe his wife wouldn't be the way she is today.'

She began to speak, then shook her head. 'No, it doesn't matter.'

'Go on.'

'I was just going to say, it seems to me that Emma's spent her life searching for a man like her father. I don't mean that as some glib, psychological summing-up. But the relationship between them was rather different from the usual father and daughter thing—closer, and yet, in a way, farther apart. Most of us have a far from adoring view of our parents, but I'm sure she adores him—adored, I should say. Doesn't it seem ludicrous that in the space of one day a change of tense should be necessary?'

'A man like her father. One couldn't exactly say that I fitted the bill. Of course, as you probably know, it was nothing more than a slip-up that led us into holy matrimony. Led *her*, I should say. I wanted to marry her, almost from the very beginning.'

She did know that—and more. She looked at him, distracted and innocent, with compassion. She thought back to that time when her jealousy of Emma had finally evaporated, to that evening of the storm when Emma had knocked at her door, because there was no other door upon which she dared knock.

'Emma? Shouldn't you be giving your inimitable interpretation of a spear-carrier, or whatever it is this week?' she'd said.

'I should. I've phoned them and told them I feel like death. Marion can do it. She does it better than me anyway.'

'But I thought this kind of weather suited your temperament. You always said the calm before the storm stimulated your hormone balance.'

'A hormone is a noise heard inside a brothel,' Emma said without humour, and moved over to the mirror where she pushed lank bunches of hair behind her ears. 'My hormone balance will never be the same again. Christ! I look awful.'

'You look as though you're getting a fever. I told you your slovenly habits would lead one day to bubonic plague.'

Emma didn't smile. 'I'm in trouble.'

'Trouble?'

'Yes, you know, trouble. Capital t trouble. Victorian melodrama trouble. I am, as they so delicately put it, in the club.'

'You're not?'

'Why is it that when anybody confronts anybody else with incontrovertible fact, their immediate reaction is to say "You're not"? Unless you can think of any other reason for nature not following its lunar course, I well and truly am. And don't look so shocked, you haven't heard the worst yet.'

So Geraldine had heard the worst—with wide-open eyes and growing amazement. Oh no. Things like that didn't happen to nicely-brought-up girls like Emma Sainter. They happened in the backs of women's magazines to be sniggered over and read aloud in ill-educated accents for effect. 'You mean you don't know whether it's John's or it's David's?' It *couldn't* be true; she must have heard wrong.

'In a nutshell.' Emma's voice was a curfew tolling the knell. Huddled in the corner of the sofa, she looked like a timid sea creature bereft of its carapace. She, who had floated immaculate through life, now cornered and trapped, ashamed, and ashamed of having to feel shame. For the first time in their lives, Geraldine sighted the target, then laid down her perfectly-poised arrows and opted for kindness.

They'd talked and talked that evening. She didn't love John any more, even if he could have married her, which he couldn't. Tell her father? Geraldine must be raving. Tell him she was pregnant and couldn't establish parenthood? Perhaps she could have done once, but not now. Somehow they didn't connect any more. And David? David would marry her.

'And don't you want to marry David?'

'Yes. No. Sometimes yes, very much. Other times not. It depends on my mood. I'd just like him to be there, without having to feel chained to him.'

'You *could* persuade yourself in time, you know, that the John incident had never happened.'

'I know. I can persuade myself about anything—for so long. I need a compass. Oh Gerry, why can't I be like you? Allergic to messes. They used to say that to me at school: "Why can't you be like Geraldine?" I hated you.'

'It was mutual.'

They'd talked and talked. Geraldine, organiser, list-maker, the most responsible girl in the class, putting forward sensible suggestions; Emma verging on hysteria, beating her fists rhythmically against her knees, 'Gerry, I need an old lady with a crochet-hook. But I'm too scared.' Or relapsing into the normal sardonic Emma: 'You wouldn't happen to have the odd hundred and fifty pounds about you? No, and if you did you'd be spending it on your bloody package tour to the Tyrol or wherever.'

The storm had finally broken and they'd resolved nothing. Geraldine had cowered while Emma ran to the window. 'You should see it. Fork *and* sheet! The sky's pink.' Then, turning, 'Things *will* work out, won't they Gerry? Won't they?'

Geraldine turned the car into the garage. She remembered to wait until David came round to open her door. If his manners were acquired and bourgeois, then she wished she knew more people whose manners were acquired and bourgeois. Things had worked out all right—for Emma. He took her arm; the path was glassy. Did you know you'd been conned? she thought. And would it make any difference if you did? Taking Emma home to meet your parents, holding her forehead while she vomited, standing up beside her before the registrar while she tightened her muscles to hold in a bulge that no one would have noticed anyway, your bulge, or so you thought. It could have been at that. Who knows? Not even Emma. At least she was spared the ordeal of watching it grow and the daily dread of looking to see who it resembled.

She put her key into the lock. The fire glowed. Pinkerton yelped. David said, 'God, Geraldine, you're lucky.'

'Lucky?'

'To be able to come home to a place that welcomes you.'

Emma had waited until a test had proved her pregnancy positive, not just a malicious foible on nature's part, before she concluded her unresolved conversation with Geraldine.

'I'm going to tell David,' she'd said. 'I've thought and I've thought and the more I think, the surer I am that it must be David's.'

Geraldine had said all sorts of things about due rewards for criminally rash behaviour—which was just the kind of comment Emma needed, implying she was some sort of tart who leapt blithely into bed with all-comers, instead of an unfortunate person who'd relied too heavily on previous good luck—then agreed that it seemed to be the best course of action as she'd left it too late for anything else.

'I still think you should have told your father.'

'He'd think I'd betrayed him. And he'd be right.'

'Betrayed him? You're mad.'

Mad or not, she'd known that there was a certain way of imparting the news to David which would induce pride and tenderness, rather than horror, and it was proved to be correct.

And, telling him, that tenderness she saw in his face proved to be reciprocal. 'How soon can we be married?' he'd said and, filled with a warm, fond gratitude that she mistook for what she thought of as love, she forgot the nights when fear, despair and disgust had plagued her alternately.

On Sunday afternoon, he took her home for tea and, quite casually, all among the willow pattern and the jam tarts, he announced that they were going to be married and rather quickly because Emma was expecting a baby.

Emma blenched, jaws clamped together in shock, she nearly broke a tooth on a chicken bone. She didn't dare to shift her eyes from Mr Campion's Adam's apple which moved up and down his throat with a mesmeric regularity. But everyone continued to eat trifle.

Eventually, his mother spoke. It wasn't the way she'd have wanted it, but you know what they said about spilt milk, and after all, she couldn't have wished for a nicer daughter-in-law.

And Emma was suddenly aware of that which had not penetrated into her obtuse brain beforehand : to Jack and Margaret Campion, nice, cosy, Jack and Margaret Campion, she with her reddened hands and home-perm, he with his silver armbands and mild Saturday flutter on the dogs, she was something of a trophy, a girl who had had a relatively posh upbringing, a symbol of David's evolution from his terraced environment. She wondered what sort of treatment would have been accorded to the erstwhile Janet had she been the one to blunder.

Afterwards, pretending to dry dishes in the kitchen,

142

Emma listened to Margaret Campion's monologue as she waved a dish mop and allowed cigarette ash to drop into the washing-up water.

'It's a shame this had to happen, but then I'm not one to sit in judgment.' She paused to pick up the cigarette end between soapy thumb and forefinger, draw the remaining gasp of life out of it, then push it through the interstices of the plug-hole. 'The same thing happened to me. You'd never think it to look at him now, but Father was quite a lad in his younger days.' The smoke-filled, faded eyes gazed through the evil yellow fish on the plastic curtains, vainly attempting to recapture the vision of old passion.

And maybe once, before the curlers and the heavy carbohydrate diet took over, Margaret Campion had been a ripe, golden, Renoir girl, but Emma's whole delicate, overwrought system recoiled from such familiar unburdening. She hadn't the slightest desire to be filed in the same category as Margaret Campion. Whatever her sins and stupidities, they were her own individual sins and stupidities. She hoped that weaning David away from his parents would not prove to be too difficult. And thinking of parents drew her on, inevitably, to the thought she'd been putting out of her head for days: that very soon she must make the journey home and somehow break the news in such a way that her father's lip would not curl in distaste.

'I must go alone,' she told David, 'or else I might never do it.'

He argued for days. It seemed that he believed, once in the bosom of her family, he would never see her again. Finally he agreed, though he would much have preferred to face her parental music himself. He saw her off at the station, bought her a lapful of unsuitable magazines and adjured her to take things quietly. Waving to his diminishing blur of face on the platform, she was overwhelmingly glad that, come what might, he would be there when she came back.

The outside of the house had been painted and the old conservatory was gone. She shivered, ready to read omens into anything. The feeling of alienation was intensified when she walked round to the back of the house and saw that the bottom of the garden, formerly a riotous paradise of undergrowth and bramble and decayed potting-sheds, had been ruthlessly chopped down and tidied to a rectangular bleakness.

Her mother was lying on a sofa reading Ivy Compton-Burnett. That, at least, was reassuring; for as long as Emma could remember, her mother had read Ivy Compton-Burnett.

They greeted each other in the over-polite way that had been their custom since Emma grew old enough to realize that their relationship was not quite the same as that between other mothers and daughters, but Emma, who had rarely regarded her mother with a feeling more complicated than impatience, after an absence of two years, was shocked by the changes in her appearance. Julia had good bone structure, nothing could alter that, but the transparent skin, stretched over her cheekbones, was beginning to develop a tracery of wrinkles and her hair, once the colour of conkers, was now quite grey. Change and decay in all around I see, Emma thought. 'What's happening to everything round here?'

'Your father is getting it all tidied up. I believe he's going to sell.'

'No! He can't sell. He mustn't.'

'Why not? He's been thinking about it for quite some time. It's far too big and it's so difficult to get help. And now he's had an offer from some people who want to turn it into flats.'

'And you don't mind?'

'Why should I mind? It's all the same to me wherever we go.'

'Oh God,' Emma said, lips turned down at the corners as they used to be when she was eight years old and couldn't get her own way. 'Oh God. Everything's becoming utterly horrible.'

Her mother merely said, 'You don't look at all well Emma. You've gone thinner. Have I said something funny?'

'No, Mother.' The smile vanished from Emma's face as quickly as it had appeared. 'Nothing funny.'

Her father didn't say, 'Emma, you don't look at all well.' He looked at her and, as she'd foreseen, he knew. Emma gazed at the amber liquid reflected in the prisms of his glass. *He* had always conducted his life with a grace of which she would never be capable.

'You're thinking of selling?' she said, looking over his shoulder at the picture of some revelling Dutch drunks who had revelled in that position for as long as she could remember. There was a stain on the edge of the frame, a souvenir from the time she'd let fly with a bottle of Indian ink during a fit of temper.

'Yes. Long overdue too. Do you object?'

'Strongly.'

'But you've never spent longer than a couple of months at a time here in the last six years.'

'I object to my stability being undermined. I want it always to be here to come back to.'

Julia Sainter book-marked her novel and carried it through to the kitchen to read while she supervised the dinner. Emma closed the door behind her. 'I'm getting married,' she said, and he said, almost in the same breath, 'I suppose you're pregnant.'

'Why is it that you know? How can you always know?'

'You're too much like me for me not to know.'

She put down her glass. Tio Pepe suddenly tasted like meths. 'This is ludicrous, isn't it? Shouldn't you be searching out your shotgun, or something equally dramatic? Perhaps I should have presented you with a *fait accompli.*'

'How long?'

'Three and a half months.'

'Why didn't you come to me earlier? It could have been arranged, so simply. God Emma, why?'

She saw what she had expected to see : the faint spasm of revulsion that crossed his features. Like a good many philanderers, he had little sympathy for those whose philandering brought them to grief.

'I daren't come and tell you.'

'Daren't?'

'You were the last person.'

He didn't pursue it; he knew what she meant. 'Why isn't the party responsible telling me all this?'

'I wouldn't let him.'

'Why not? Isn't he presentable? Are you now going to add the *coup de grâce* by telling me he's not the sort you can bring home?'

Perhaps that was the moment, fleeting though it was, when she might have slipped into banter and said, 'Actually, he's only what they call the putative father. Dear old Dad, tell me what to do.' But *his* flippancy was the sort born out of reaction to shock and her tongue would not form the words.

'Do you *want* to marry him?'

'I think I do. I'm very, very fond of him. And he's always wanted to marry me and wants the baby and everything.' For the first time she looked full into his face. He had never appeared so old. And for the first time she realized the consequences of her action affected other people too. On her knees beside him, she sobbed into his coat sleeve while he pushed wet strands of hair out of her eyes just as he had done the day she forgot her lines in the Christmas play and the time she was brought home from school with jaundice.

'Oh Emma,' he said. 'Why did you have to learn from experience? And have you learned? People like you and me —perhaps we never do.'

'Would you like some music?' Geraldine said, happening by chance upon a record in a faded and tattered cover which, in the florid hand she was favouring during that period, proclaimed Emma's ownership. Bloody Emma everywhere. As if it wasn't enough that she should be wrecking people's lives at a distance.

David craned his neck, reading upside down. 'Schumann? Anything but that. Whenever Schumann goes on to the record player, I know the wind's in the east.'

So Emma still clung to the signature tunes of her love affairs, placed the needle on the record and remembered something she'd probably kidded herself might have been.

Mendelssohn, at any rate, seemed to be association-free for him. She sat down at the other end of the sofa. Getting dark outside already. Really she ought to put on the light, but the fire was cosier. Sometimes, in her sillier moments, she used to dream up situations like this; the only difference was that in her dreams the man occupying the other end of the sofa was faceless and available; this one was Emma's husband and was leaving at six o'clock.

He followed her eyes to the clock. 'Two hours,' he said. 'And then I enter the realm of decision. Why can't time be like a piece of elastic? Stretch it for the good times and let it contract for the bad.'

'I suppose the least I can say is that I shall never agree to send spurious invitations again.'

He appreciated just how much effort had been needed to enunciate those words. And he was surprised that whatever desire he might have had to make her suffer for her part in the deception had evaporated entirely. 'You're a nice girl Geraldine,' he said.

Which was not the right thing to say. She flushed. 'Emma always used to say "I expect she has a nice nature. In fact she'd *have* to have a nice nature," about any girl who had no physical attributes to recommend her.'

'I'm not Emma.'

Perhaps it was the firelight, or his own state of mind, or a combination of both, but suddenly he saw her. Not differently. Just, for the first time, actually saw her. Had never seen her before without Emma, therefore had only thought of her as being all the things Emma was not.

He'd spent twenty-four hours involving her, against her will, in his marital troubles; he'd got drunk and said foolish things to her and despite all that she'd remained sympathetic, but more than that—straight.

He was tempted to ask why she'd remained friendly with Emma, but before he could voice the question he realized he knew the answer to it. It was not a matter of her remaining friendly with Emma; it was Emma who clung tenaciously to the friendship. Because, in Geraldine, Emma would see those qualities she pretended not to admire, qualities like strength and purpose and constancy. Perhaps, obsessed with Emma and influenced by Emma's mocking lack of philosophy, he'd forgotten that once he'd admired those qualities too.

There'd been a moment last night when, if she had given him the slightest encouragement, he'd have made sure that he wouldn't be relegated to the spare bedroom. Thank God that moment had gone unchallenged and unanswered. The idea of using anyone to work out his bitterness was abhorrent to him, and to have used her, he saw quite clearly now, would have been unforgivable.

Today, a lot of things seemed different. Suspended from the necessity to make decisions, he felt, quite simply, safe. To stay here, safe from crises, safe from betrayals—

She stood up and reached across him for the ashtray. She could have asked him to pass her the ashtray. He caught and held her searching hand. His grasp asked for comfort, for help, his grasp said please don't send me back to Emma—just yet.

She stood in front of him, off-balance, unable to look anywhere but straight at him. So this was what they meant when they said there comes a moment—no matter whether it comes after you've known each other a respectable length of time, or if it happens when you cross a threshold and see a stranger. She could move backwards, pretend he'd put out a hand to steady her, or she could move forwards. She'd almost forgotten that feeling that's like melting inside, the feeling that vanishes utterly from the consciousness until it's recalled by someone else. It seemed as though they'd been immobilized for a year. For the first time in her life she postponed analysis until after the event. She moved forwards.

Inside his arms she was at first awkward. It had been some time since the last man and, as with other pursuits that have not been recently practised, readjustment comes only gradually. The taste and smell of him were just as some unconscious precognition had told her they would be. They were kissing—deliberate, no-nonsense kissing. Her thoughts were racing too fast for her to make sense of them. Oh Emma, your husband is kissing me, burying his head in my neck, clinging to me and clutching me, asking for the warmth and reality you can't or won't give him. All our lives Emma you've taken from me, not always because you've wanted what I had, but just for the victory of taking it. Well every dog has its day and now it's my turn. But Emma, this time I'm surer of victory than ever you could have been. You'd say he's come to me because he can't have you; in essence it may be true, but that explanation is a little too facile. He's come to me because I can give him the dignity you've robbed him of. And, in paying you back, his eyes will gradually open and he'll be astounded that he could have allowed himself to play the degraded role you allotted to him for so long.

He raised his face from the smoothness of her shoulder. She'd been prepared to find it beautiful; she was not disappointed. 'I never cared much for struggling on sofas,' he said.

It would have been so easy to do an Emma, to invest the moment with the intensity of a lifetime. Native caution reasserted itself in time. Without moving her lips from his temple hair, she told him that neither of them was equipped with the armour so necessary for those who live on their emotions. You saw them everywhere, the people who'd succumbed to an impression, then spent the rest of their lives avoiding each other. Did he want that to happen?

He raised himself into a sitting position, pulling her with him. Automatically, she lifted a hand to adjust her dress, smooth her hair. He lowered it. 'We're not being watched. You're not the woman taken in adultery. That role belongs to someone else.'

'Precisely,' she said.

He cupped her face in his hands; the pressure of his thumbs was such that he might almost have wanted to obliterate it from his view. 'I told you yesterday that I haven't the talent for casual lusts—games—I wish to God I had.'

'Which means?'

'Which means that I couldn't treat you as a female body in which to drown myself, even if I wanted to—which I don't.'

'So we could—make love and so you'd go home thinking well, at least she was glad of it, and I'd sit here rejecting each acceptable explanation for our actions that presented itself. People talk about degrees of adultery, but I don't believe it. The difference between making love and not making love can't be measured.'

He was stroking her hair, tangling his fingers in it, but he seemed to be unaware that he was doing so. 'Do you want me?'

'Yes.' It didn't seem that there was any other possible answer.

'Then whether we make love at this moment or six months hence is immaterial. Can't you understand that? You're quite right when you tell me that, once apart, we'll both start to rationalize and being two sensible people, we'll probably decide not to. But it won't be a decision that calls for congratulation; it'll be the decision of two people who are afraid to give of themselves.'

'Why should I allow myself to be hurt—again? Whatever anyone says, to give is not enough—unless you're a saint. Besides—'

'What you were going to say is that besides, that's exactly what Emma's doing. But it isn't, you know. There's a difference between giving and gambling.'

She freed her hand, stood up and switched on the light. Let him tell her all this in the far from gentle glow of a hundred-watt electricity bulb. He watched her fiddling with cigarette and lighter, movements tense and jerky; she was not the same woman who had relaxed against him a moment ago. But she could be again. He had no doubts about that.

'Yesterday,' she said, the cool impersonal voice from the classroom dais, 'you came here and you discovered that your wife had been lying to you. Perhaps you were prepared for that knowledge, but there's a world of difference between suspecting and knowing. At any rate, you reacted, reacted in the way that anyone in your position would have done, a position that is of the partner who is beyond reproach. Today, for whatever combination of reasons, you wish to reverse that position. It's only when there's no need to reverse positions that you could even begin to think of wanting anyone.'

'I daresay if you get down to fundamentals, everything can be reduced to an equation. I suppose what you're trying to say, in your admirably neutral way, is that it's not until I don't want Emma any more that I have any right to invade your life.' In front of the mirror he restored his tie to its moorings, pulled down his cuffs. 'You're absolutely right. With one mess to contend with, I should have more sense than to start perpetrating another one.'

Through the mirror he watched her face. He didn't think he'd ever seen a face so incapable of dissimulation. After years with Emma he'd forgotten that women were, after all, members of the same species. 'You don't really want me to go home and pretend this never happened, do you?'

'If you want to be free. If, when you do get home, you take a long look and still want to be free, then I should like you to be free.'

But freedom was not what he wanted. Sometimes, coming home from work, he'd look into some lighted window and see warmth and laughter and comfort, and feel that life through that window must be very different from his own. A delusion of course; probably the occupants had just finished having a white-hot row—or were just preparing for one. Being in this room was as if he'd passed through to the other side of one of those windows and found that it did, after all, match up to his expectations. Here it seemed as though everything belonged, as though there was a loving affinity between each object and its owner. Some people expressed their personality through their possessions, just as other people—Emma—refused to be stabilized by or attached to their belongings, regarding it in some way as a loss of freedom.

'You must go.'

'Yes, I must go.' He put his hand on her arm. Despite the last few minutes, a more intimate gesture would somehow have seemed improper. He realized that for her to even contemplate anything long-term, she had to be convinced that she was essential to him. 'I've found something here, Geraldine.'

'Yes,' she said. 'Sanctuary. But sanctuary was only supposed to be a temporary state of affairs, wasn't it?'

Emma was filing her nails into regular, flawless oval shapes. Patrick was checking through some figures. Not as a result of a fit of pique this time, but because the covering of *his* tracks entailed being able to show something for his visit and also because he wanted to do it anyway.

He was totally absorbed, flicking over page after page and tapping his cigarette on the edge of the ashtray. She reflected that three days, well, three nights actually, away from one's routine existence contained the same number of hours which had to be filled somehow. Their previous encounters had been pathetically, horribly, brief; it was only now she was discovering just how easy it might be for boredom to creep in. *She* wasn't bored, but you couldn't tell with Patrick. Someone always on the go as he was would be bound to get bored more quickly than a slow-motion person like herself. You could make love for only a certain

amount of the time, and talking could be dangerous. It was
a bit like a honeymoon when the weather's bad. She remembered her own honeymoon : Southern Ireland, one of
those converted Halls of Tara, all gargoyles and studded
doors three feet thick, looking out of the bridal chamber
down to a lake in which a betrayed maiden was reputed to
have drowned herself some three hundred years ago. How it
had rained! The centre of their universe should have been
the four-poster, draped vulgarly in blue satin, but there
were few unique experiences for them to discover; pots of
tea, brewed so strong it was almost red, carried up to them
by a timid young chambermaid, straight out of the Convent
of the Sacred Heart. And outside, wherever they went,
wimples by the score : Sisters Teresa, Luke and Peter Paul
on a cultural spree, frisking a little, between bells. Had she
and David been of the right persuasion, they might have
been able to occupy their time more easily; as it was, they
stuck it out for a week, pretending everything was lovely,
and then, each seeing through the other's pretence, collapsed laughing on the vast bed and packed their cases for
home, post-haste. One of the infrequent times when they
had been totally in sympathy with each other.

She put her nail-file away. Half an hour perhaps, until
they could dine. Would he never finish his work? The room
offered few distractions : a notice advising guests to lock
their valuables in the safe, a pamphlet advertising a night-
club, a telephone directory, a bible. Perhaps a chapter or
two of Exodus, a musing upon the relevant command-
ments? I must remember to bring a book next time, she
thought. Then she thought I must not make optimistic
assumptions like 'next time'; far better to reflect upon our
good fortune in managing these three nights, when formerly
we had to be content with an afternoon or an evening in a

flat belonging to a friend of his called Paul Maxwell whom
I have never met but who must be the most accommodating
man on earth, or perhaps charges a small fee, or perhaps is
being nice to Patrick in order to attain promotion. Just
like that film. What was it called? Lousy recall for black and
white facts. Must embark upon one of those memory courses
that change your whole life for you.

She'd brushed her hair with three hundred strokes,
smoked two cigarettes and recited the only verse of 'Ode to
a Nightingale' she could remember, twice over, before he
snapped his briefcase shut.

'Thank God that's out of the way.'

'What will you do, Patrick,' she said, pulling frayed
threads from the edge of her dressing-gown sleeve, 'when
you've become what you want to become and there are no
summits left to aim for? Will you concentrate on money, or
maintaining your power, or will you take off for a retreat in
the country where you'll do nothing more ambitious than
trout-fish or hoe the potatoes?'

'I'll probably have a coronary at forty-five and never
have to face that problem.'

'No!' She'd gone quite pale. 'There's nothing wrong with
you, is there?'

'No. I was only joking.'

'Then don't joke about that kind of thing.'

'I can see,' he said, 'that we shall have to work on your
sense of humour. Persuade you to see the lighter side.'

Other people have tried, she thought. And failed. I don't
find many things about life amusing, unless you regard the
whole experience as a bloody meaningless farce.

'It's getting muggy in here.' He opened the window and
leaned out.

'If it wasn't that you're lovely and warm to sleep with,'
she said, 'I would have nothing more to do with you.

I've always fled for my life from the good brisk walk, plenty of fresh air type like you.'

'You're a dormouse. A natural hibernator. Like someone we once lived next door to who took to his bedroom in November and stayed there till March.'

'What did he do? How did he live? Wasn't he bored?'

'He was financially able to do it and he had an obliging wife who was rather proud of his eccentricity. I believe he occupied the time with huge, enormously complicated jig-saw puzzles and read his way through Harrods' library.'

'You know,' she said, 'I rather admire that. Obviously he didn't give a damn about what people thought. He might have had a secret desire to travel up the Amazon, and if he had, everyone would have praised him for it, but instead he preferred to retire to bed and develop his mental faculties, regardless of ridicule. What happened to him?'

'He was run over by a Green Line bus.'

'You're having me on!'

'No I'm not. It was in May.'

'Which proves something.'

'It probably proves you're never entirely safe at any time after leaving the womb.'

She joined him beside the window. 'Look at them, all those little ants rushing out of their various ant-heaps, looking ever so important, half a pint in the pub and then home to Mary's dried-up coq-au-vin. *They'd* never dare to take to their beds. They only exist by imagining themselves through other people's eyes.'

'They're necessary.'

'Being necessary just isn't enough.'

'Oh yes it is,' he said emphatically. 'This world wouldn't stop turning if you or I ceased to be, but take away that army of little men, cogs in big wheels, and total collapse would ensue. They do their humdrum jobs, in the main, uncomplainingly. Their rewards are small, so are their hopes, but we need them, they represent order.'

'And is order so necessary?'

'Naturally. At least I've never heard yet of an anarchist state functioning satisfactorily.'

'So, as long as we all obey the law, practise monogamy, produce two-point-whatever-it-is children, fence off our individual minute areas and never stop to ask why, things will continue to function?'

'More or less. Utopia was precisely that—a dream.'

'It makes me sick,' she said, grinding out her cigarette. 'Everybody makes me sick. Sitting and moaning about the narrowness of life, but conforming so rigidly as to ensure it gets narrower. Whereas the people who actually do what they want, regardless, are thought of as being quite beyond the pale.'

'You've put your finger on it—regardless—that's why they *are* mostly beyond the pale. They have no regard for whoever they might be hurting in the process of getting what they want. Anyway, why are you so vehement about it?'

She closed the window and pulled her dressing-gown tight around her. She looked like the defender of a lost cause. 'They talked about my father, all those old bitches whispering over the bridge-tables and the cream-cakes. When they ran out of half-truths, they fabricated entirely. Because he had the courage to seek after his pleasures. Because he could no longer love my mother and needed to love someone. They'd have harmed him, the little jealous men in the board-room or the golf club, but he was too powerful and too detached for them to harm him, so they talked about him instead. Probably they still do. Because they know he's bigger than they are, conceived on a larger scale, won't

conform to their puerile, locker-room ideas of morality,
because he can't just lust, he has to try to love.'

She sank on to the bed, quite out of breath. 'That's why
all your little, necessary, safe men make me want to vomit.'

He scratched the side of his face. 'And what about your
mother?'

'My mother should have had the good grace to release
him from responsibility.'

'I'm just not qualified to argue with you,' he said. 'I grew
up in a normal home. My father and mother seemed to be
reasonably happy with each other. If either of them had
their adventures, then they were discreet about them.'

'You mean they were dishonest.'

'I mean they were discreet. They provided a safe, stable
background for me and consequently I grew into a normal,
orderly sort of chap, concerned just to keep people happy.'

'How the hell can you judge that?' she said, making a
face of disgust. 'How do you know your wife's happy?
Perhaps she cries at night when you're asleep. How do you
know I'm happy? People don't come straight out and tell
you they're unhappy, because they feel it's a reflection upon
their own adequacy.'

'I hope I don't make you unhappy.'

Why should you imagine you've ever made me unhappy,
she thought, what evidence have I ever given you? You'll
never know about those awful dead days when you were ill
and I thought it was over between us, or when you took
Beryl to Italy and I was in damp, miserable England, trying
my hardest not to think of you making love to her in some
hot room behind closed shutters. My father, at least, doesn't
give his women those grounds for jealousy.

He folded his arms round her. 'Let me make you happy.'

Sometimes he could look so sincerely hurt: frown lines,
candid eyes, long black lashes. She stroked his face, adjusted

the knot in his tie, traced a kiss on to his lips with her finger. 'You should be put out to stud.'

'Actually I meant a drink. The bar should be open now. Take you down for a drink, sit you on a bar stool beside me and have every other man in the place wild with jealousy.' He picked up his jacket.

'Let me get dressed first. If I go down like this, they might get wild with something else.'

She picked a blue dress out of the wardrobe. Her best one. Pale blue velvet embroidered with gold round the collar. She'd deliberately saved her most stunning impression for this last evening. The dress, and the shoes that had cost so much she'd burned the bill before David could see it and say, 'That would have kept one starving Biafran in food for five years.' Not that he was a mean man; it was just that he thought clothes should be useful investments, not just things to be dressed up in before the wardrobe mirror when you felt low; could never understand the feeling you got when buying a new dress, the feeling that with that new dress, a whole new life would be opened up for you.

Getting heated had ruined her make-up. She removed it and started again from scratch. 'I'm sorry,' she said, 'but I look a wreck.'

'You look gorgeous, but if that's not your opinion, go ahead and re-do the whole thing. I love watching women dress anyway.'

'Through keyholes of course, for preference. Peeping Patrick. The scourge of the ladies' dormitory.'

'You know what I mean. I love the awkwardness they display: fumbling with straps and zips and buttons, biting their lower lips and clenching their teeth and contorting their faces just to get a bit of eye-black in the right place. Then those terribly nonchalant dabs of scent here and there, and the way they get up, looking so uncertain and

159

can never resist that final glance just in case something's collapsed during the second since they moved away from the mirror.'

'Only because women, by and large, have so little confidence in their appearance. One glance in the morning for a man and he's all right for the rest of the day. But women have to look in shop windows, car windows, any reflecting surface, continually, just to make sure they're fit to face the world. There.' She turned to face him. 'Was it worth waiting for?'

'You should never wear anything but blue,' he said. 'It reflects back into your eyes.'

A man good with compliments. Was it natural or was it the result of practice? How many women who looked good in blue, how many perfumes had there been before he was able to deliver such phrases with grace and assurance? How many typists, women colleagues, were there, with neat little bottoms and clear skin and newly-washed hair, ready to steal him from her? How on earth did Beryl cope?

'You look beautiful.'

'Thank you,' she said. But she knew, in the long run, it wasn't of much value.

David swung the car into the endless monotony of the motorway, switching the radio through station after station in the hope that one of them was broadcasting some enthralling play that would distract his thoughts. None of them were. The road conditions were still bad and for miles he drove in second, contemplating the registration plate of the Herald in front of him whose occupants appeared to be young, very young, a boy and a girl with leopard-skin cushions and a dangling distraction in the back window, who could not refrain from touching one another. Once, he saw the blonde curtain of hair fall sideways as she leaned across to be kissed. He remembered a facetious article he'd read in some newspaper which listed thirty-five excuses a wife could have at the ready to refuse her husband's advances. He was familiar with all of them. It was a long, long time since Emma had turned her cheek towards him as they drove along a clear stretch of road. Or had he only ever imagined it?

So difficult to think back to the beginning, but there had, undoubtedly, been good things. Even if a miscarriage wasn't exactly the best thing with which to start off married life. 'Have another child, as soon as possible,' the doctor had advised when Emma was weeping in corners and saying that it was a judgment upon her for making him marry her. Which was arrant nonsense, he'd said, as there'd been no make about it. 'Have another child.' And she was as anxious as he, if only, it seemed to him, to justify the marriage. But nothing had come of it. It seemed that Emma could only conceive at a time that wasn't propitious.

She'd recovered, though. He remembered Emma in the brand new house, the deposit paid for out of a cheque her father had given them, like a small girl pretending to be grown up, playing with shiny copper saucepans and tins of paint, hemming miles of curtaining by hand, lips pursed and a deep line etched between her eyebrows; he remembered those curtains, hanging, different lengths, each side of the french windows. She'd howled for half an hour. The house was her plaything. She scoured glossy magazines for room plans, sat up into the night experimenting with colour schemes, got him to build a shelf in the kitchen to house her collection of cookery books, most of the recipes in which would have flummoxed Escoffier. He'd been surprised that she could relinquish what he thought of as her career apparently without a qualm, though he was glad of it. 'No, it doesn't bother me too much,' she'd said. 'I was never any good at it. Come to that, I was never very good at anything. Perhaps I'll make a brilliant housewife.' But the initial love affair with domesticity gradually began to pall. One evening, instead of being warned to wipe his feet before he walked on the kitchen floor, he found the kitchen floor hadn't been washed and Emma curled up on a sofa reading about fertility.

The doctor's surgery became her substitute for compulsive housework. She was convinced that something must have gone wrong when she had the miscarriage. The doctor, with a waiting-room full of women who were unwillingly pregnant for the fourth or fifth time, suggested she visit a specialized clinic. But two visits to *that* place were sufficient for her. 'How many times and in what position!' she told him when she came back, still red-faced with the indignity of it. 'And an awful female doctor with a lisp and a moustache showing me horrid little diagrams. I couldn't.'

So she didn't. And put the fertility books in a trunk up in the lumber room.

Sexually, he thought everything was all right. It was good for him; he assumed it was as good for her, being too reticent to put questions into words. He'd been shattered the night she said crisply and petulantly, 'Oh *must* you take so long about it?' He didn't know anybody could be that cruel. It was after that he took out a well-made, willing wench from the typing pool, intending to assert his virility, but finding, when it came to the point, he'd rather not after all. He thought of other men he knew who would have revenged themselves for such a blow to their masculine pride by having it off with every girl available. He didn't want available girls, he wanted Emma. And he continued to have her, but he couldn't help feeling that it was on her terms, as though some lunar regularity drove her to seek release and he just happened to be the convenient man for the job.

How long was it before he resigned himself to the short-comings of the relationship? Two years? Three years? Steadily he climbed the ladder of professional success. Within the limits of his nine to five existence, he was sharp, precise, in control, to his colleagues a man who didn't know he was born, having a wife like that, because Emma, in social respects, was never to be found wanting. She'd bribe the cleaning woman to stay on and cook fancy dinners, deliberately dress herself to eclipse the other wives who tried desperately, but never quite achieved the same effect and then be found drinking in the kitchen with somebody's enchanted husband. The women disliked her, the men adored her and Emma, when they'd gone home, mimicked all of them mercilessly and said how could there be so many boring people in one firm.

A few of her old art school friends were still to be found, living their perpetual adolescence. He regarded them, with their contrived artiness, their jeering, their mistresses and squalid residences, as a joke. At least he felt safer when she was with them than when she was entertaining his own colleagues who, though they might be boring, were more conventionally lecherous.

It was due to one of these old acquaintances, a yellow-faced designer in velveteen trousers, called Robinson, just Robinson, which was in itself disconcerting, whom she'd bumped into quite by chance, that she began to draw again. From that point things began to move rapidly. She was commissioned to illustrate a children's book. It was a great success. Others followed. Not that he'd objected—at first; if it gave her a *raison d'être*, then he was happy enough. The feeling that he was standing on quicksand came later. Portfolio in arms, climbing into a taxi, she was no longer just Mrs Campion, she was again Emma in her own right. Discussing it, she said that at last she felt fulfilled, but he knew that it was not the execution of clever, fashionably-distorted drawings that made her feel fulfilled, it was the excitement of being drawn back into the whirl, the parade of attractive faces who, by virtue of their expense accounts, could gaze with pleasure at her newly-animated features. And, with him, she was willing to share her new life only to a certain extent; it was as if she treasured it as something apart from him, a reassurance that a part of her existed and laughed and was admired on an entirely different plane.

Still, that was all right too. The cleaning woman left. Dust powdered the expensive surfaces of the house and a cobweb or two laced its way around the light fitments while she, tongue creeping out of her mouth and face smudged with charcoal, drew and painted and groaned and dashed crumpled paper to the floor with an obscenity or stepped back with an awed smile to survey something that had, miraculously, come right. All of the nagging irritations : the periodic domestic chaos, the fruitlessness of trying to communicate with somebody totally absorbed in the creative act, he could stand. As for her new circle of acquaintanceship : he had long been of the opinion that Emma was one of those women who, requiring admiration as they require food and drink, gain their satisfaction from the titillation of flirting. It was only during the last couple of months that he'd begun to doubt his assessment. Just superficial signs : their sexual relationship, hitherto far from frequent but at least regular, tailing off almost to abstention and, once or twice, the postman arriving before he'd left for work, bearing a letter in an unfamiliar hand which was not left lying around as her other letters were left lying around. A surreptitious search when she was out, despising himself as he opened drawers and rooted inside them, yielded nothing either. It was the phone call that clinched it. He was off work with a heavy cold when the phone rang and, actress though she may have been, she wasn't *that* good an actress —she'd have been the first to admit it.

His first, natural reaction had been the desire to punch whoever-he-was on the nose, his second was to try to imagine what sort of man Emma might choose, unaware that it was a matter of her being chosen; he lay awake, sifting his meagre evidence, evidence which could be arranged either to condemn her or to establish her innocence, depending upon his mood. The obvious course of action, to ask her outright, he rejected because, hideous though this uncertainty was, it was preferable to having to watch her lie to him.

And what now? He gazed, without comprehension, at a giant blue and white sign. Geraldine. A name that had meant little and now meant so much. Driving to the garage, they'd exchanged hardly a word. Both of them knew that there were so many million words to be said which they were not qualified to say. By the side of three petrol pumps, surrounded by pools of melted snow, he'd pulled her close to him. She'd turned her head away, not for reasons of coquetry, or because of an upsurge of false morality; it was something that went much deeper than that. He'd kissed her anyway and, for just a second, she'd let him. Perhaps it was a foretaste of what could be, perhaps they'd never get beyond that foretaste. 'I'm going to write to you,' he'd said. Said it like a threat.

'Perhaps.'

'And when this business is sorted out, I'm coming back to see you.'

'I'm not an alternative. I'm me.'

He understood what she meant, but found it difficult to

be as categorical. Alternatives: it seemed to him that that was what life was all about; who knew what lay in wait down the paths you didn't take, the parties you didn't attend? My marriage is grinding to a halt, he thought, and not being the kind of man who can support solitude, I need some one else. Therefore, my sweet Geraldine, you are my alternative. Nothing in the rules though to say you can't love the alternative more than you loved the original choice.

Another sign, which seemed to indicate that there remained only a relatively few miles until all his concentration must be focused on plotting a course through the hell on wheels that was London. The car in front now was a Mini-Cooper, ready to dart, showing off, in and out of the bigger, smoother metal monsters. Somewhere along the way the Herald must have turned off into a secluded haven for two yellow-haired lovers. How soon before *they* murdered each other? In the glove compartment, Emma's cigarettes, on the back seat *Les Fleurs du Mal* in the original, borrowed from some library when she'd decided to improve her mind. It was all he had of her—possessions: and possessions to her, he knew, were meaningless externals. If she went, she'd take only the necessities with her. He would be left among the jars and the bottles and the lengths of chocolate box ribbon, all those things that had shaped her for him. And perhaps, if they stayed together, the only parts of her that would really belong to him, bought by him for her, would be those same externals.

Tonight she would probably telephone. He did not know what he would say. He did not know to what extent either of them was equipped to make the sacrifice of pride. And whether that sacrifice would be worthwhile anyway.

Luton, the sign said, in massive capitals. As if it being

Luton should make any difference. He drove on, towards an empty house and a telephone, towards he knew not what.

Emma picked up the telephone receiver and put it down again. She wondered how many times in her life she'd been guilty of *that* indecision. 'I'll ring him after dinner.' She called Patrick back from the door. 'And remind me to recompense you when it comes to bill-time.'

'What?' He grinned, only gradually apprehending her meaning.

'Well it's hardly cricket to ring up one's husband at one's lover's expense, is it?'

Brittle, shock phrases used for effect. Never choose a soft expression if a harsh one can be found instead. As if determined to remind herself that their relationship was wrong.

This time in the dining-room there were no Dorothys and Normans to be made mock of. Just a series of identical commercial travellers sitting at their separate tables and flicking over the pages of their paperbacks, covert glances above Ellery Queen and John O'Hara. Deprived of sources for fantasy, Emma transformed her napkin from a cocked hat to a water-lily and finally to a crumpled mess. 'I have talents, as you can see,' she said.

They ordered. Or rather he ordered. She said that such an enormous menu made her neurotically indecisive. Besides, with all due respect to his wallet, she didn't care much what she ate. 'I'm cheap to keep,' she said, frivolously, finding it impossible to acknowledge the fact that tonight was their last night until neither of them knew when.

'You don't need any other talents than the one you have,' he said, anxious to maintain the flippancy.

'In fact,' she said, scoring the tablecloth with the tip of her knife, 'in fact, I have no real talents. That's always been the trouble. I'm like the man in the Bible. I had a few small sparks which never caught fire through not being diligently tended, or perhaps they never caught fire because they weren't substantial enough in the first place.'

'You draw well, you know you do.'

'The term is facility. I have a certain facility which is set between fixed limits. I'm like Branwell Brontë, or Dante Gabriel Rossetti, my gifts are too diffuse to come to anything. And the thing is, I've always had to pretend that I never had aspirations. It gained me an only partly justified reputation for not caring.'

'You really are an all-or-nothing person, aren't you?' It seemed to him that as soon as he glimpsed one facet of her personality, it swung back into darkness and another was presented to him.

'Yes,' she said simply and honestly. 'And I act in direct opposition to my beliefs. Gerry always had me labelled as a schizoid masochist, if that means anything to you.'

'I doubt whether it would have meant anything to Freud,' he said. 'I think that you and your funny friend Geraldine spent far too much time cataloguing each other.'

'But we felt it was necessary.' She emphasized each word with a tap of her melon fork against the side of her plate. 'After all, *everybody* pins labels on everybody else. There just doesn't seem to be room in life for more than one label for each person. Either someone is kind, or he's selfish, or he's neurotic. Never a hyphenated label. *We* were merely attempting to search out accurate, comprehensive ones.'

'Dear, impossible-to-label Emma, I love you. I love all the bits of everybody else and the bit that is you and nobody else, all the bits that go to make up Emma.' The more he said it, the truer it became.

She pushed away the half-eaten melon—such phrases were food and drink to her—and took his hand. Above the candle flame their fingers mingled, his supple, well-manicured, as smooth as a woman's, hers slim, slightly unkempt with traces of paint ingrained into the cuticle. 'Would I ever tire of touching you?' she said.

'In time, yes, I suppose so.'

'You mean that if we could be together, in time our marriage would become just like the ones we're seeking to escape from now? No, I refuse to believe it. If being apart means that we retain the freshness of it, then perhaps I prefer it this way.'

'I can't tell you how it would compare with your existing marriage because I don't know the *state* of your existing marriage. Except that I assume it's like mine—there's an indefinable lack of something.'

The waiter had put on a perfect cabaret performance in serving their Steak Diane; for all the effect it had on Emma, he might as well have opened a tin of beans. 'Would you say,' she commented, watching a wine stain spreading across the pristine tablecloth like pseudopodia, 'that my marriage is not successful because I'm perpetually bored, or that boredom is the result of my unsuccessful marriage?'

Then, unable to resist it : 'Is Beryl bored?'

Beryl bored? No, not bored. A lot of things, but not bored. 'She has the business of course.'

Of course. Beryl and her dress shop. That much she knew. Beryl chic and businesslike, competent among the audits and accounts, admonishing salesgirls, Beryl combining efficiency in both work and marriage.

'The ghastly thing,' she said, 'ghastly for me at any rate, is that I believe there is nothing radically wrong with your marriage. You're one of those nice, honourable men we used to read about in French novels who kept a wife and a mistress most harmoniously and with great affection and dignity.'

'Back to categorizing. Those days, when a woman was

169

either a wife or a mistress, are over. Surely we are all, in our naïveté, searching for a woman who combines both roles.'

'And perhaps there are some women who are only cut out to be one or the other. And perhaps I'm one of the ones who are cut out to be the other.'

He began to laugh, but she silenced him with a gesture. 'I'm serious. For, as I see it, your marriage is fundamentally sound. I'm just something added to your life.' Again she silenced his automatic protestation. 'I'm not deliberately denigrating myself. I daresay you love me, but you love me for being an extra. Probably you go back to Beryl that much happier for seeing me. Whereas for me, you are a clear-cut substitute, the somebody in my life who makes existence worthwhile.'

He sat forward and folded his hands. 'All right, if we're going to be analytical, what changes would you make, if it were possible to make changes?'

'If I knew, I'd make them. I *think* I'd like to throw myself completely into a constant relationship with you. Yet I'd want him to be there in case you hurt me.'

'Good God. Is it a father or a husband you want?'

'I want both I suppose. And it seems that I have to choose between one and the other.'

'One is supposed to have grown gracefully from needing a father to wanting a lover by the end of one's adolescence.'

'Then perhaps if I made the break to go to a man I couldn't be sure of, the transition might be effected.'

'Is it really so awful with him?' His first direct question amid a morass of amateur psychology.

'No, it's not awful. It's nothing, purposeless. Every day merging into the next. I've even reached the point when I'm no longer irritated by him and being irritated at least used to be some sort of a reaction, even though it was my neuroses that caused me to be irritated, rather than any fault of his.'

How well he understood her meaning : if she gives that little, dry, nervous cough just once more, if she encircles her left wrist with her right hand again, I shall leave home. Once, those involuntary actions had spelled magic, opening doors to her secret self. After five years with Emma, would the sight of her raising a glass to her lips and replacing it without drinking drive him to screaming pitch?

'If only I had some real cause for complaint, but I haven't. The whole is compounded out of a series of trifling aggravations. If I didn't know that he's a soul almost entirely without malice, I would believe that he set out deliberately to annoy : he'll go for an hour without speaking, then I'll put on some music, music to be listened to, not background, and he'll immediately strike up a conversation. Or he'll defend some dreary, *thick* friend of his to death instead of being normal and indulging in a little harmless bitchiness. I hate to admit it, but our failure is based on nothing more dramatic than my inability to tolerate him. I hate to admit it because it makes everything— the beginning, when things *might* have been good—meaningless.'

The candles were burning down. Hot wax rolled ponderously into the holders, evoking so many childhood Christmases when the hands of the clock seemed exasperatingly motionless; the clock on the wall opposite, bold, yet congruous among the sporting prints of bygone ages, would have told them, had they dared to look, that the horses of the night were galloping their time away. Emma, one of life's born fiddlers, decapitated a papery everlasting flower and said, looking away, 'Is it just that I was ready to love and you were there ready to love me? Say no. Please say no.'

'No.' He could say it and mean it. Surely that initial current of recognition, that signal, making his whole body acknowledge something lost and found, must be attributed to a force more profound than coincidence?

'Not like that?' She indicated with her head a couple who'd just come into the restaurant. Now *there* was a dirty weekend, if ever you saw one—well, dirty middle-of-the-week at any rate. The girl allowed herself to be seated, received a menu, accepted a cigarette, without once raising her eyes from the tablecloth. The man was talking loudly, joking with the waiter, over-compensating madly; any moment now he'd say 'My wife and I.'

'Christ no.' He shuddered.

'Even if they *were* in love, they'd be ashamed about it. Why should it be that there's something in us that is afraid to acknowledge love, so that we have to invent a thousand derisive or derogatory expressions with which to sneer at it?'

'Questions Emma. If I could answer them my permanent address would be Delphi. I've said I love you. And those words speak themselves, against all my logic and better judgment. Right now I want to take you to bed and stop talking.'

They walked the length of the restaurant; they did not speak or touch, but they exuded and were painfully aware that they were exuding it, the brave and blatant knowledge that they were lovers.

Where did reality begin and end? That was the question. Logically, it would seem that reality was at home with Beryl, but somehow, despite one's initial clear-headed intentions, things began to overlap, and reality could just as well consist of walking through these plasterboard Corinthian columns with Emma. A danger signal, he knew. One can be totally inexperienced in a situation and yet still recognize the danger signals. He looked at the couple they'd talked about: in between great forkfuls, the man was looking straight through the girl's eyes, being heavily, quietly, sincere. No danger of him not keeping things in their correct pigeon-holes. Patrick held open the door. My trouble, he thought, is that somewhere, deep down, there's a little bit of human being left and it won't stop trying to raise its ugly head.

Geraldine took three aspirins and closed her eyes. From childhood, nervous tension had manifested itself at a physical level; she'd graduated from asthmatic attacks, through eczema, to these appalling headaches which she supposed if she dignified them with a visit to the doctor would be diagnosed as migraine. Like wearing blinkers, someone had defined the sensation, writing about it in one of the posh women's magazines which were occasionally to be found lying around the staffroom. The same someone had also said it meant you were extraordinarily perceptive, super-sensitive, or something. Fine consolation. The last evening of my holiday and I have to spend it looking out of one eye in the middle of my head. If I still have the right to say damn you Emma, then, damn you Emma.

She picked up a novel, threw it down, reached for a school textbook—ridiculous even to think of trying to read in this condition—switched on the radio: the 'Holberg Suite'—something edgy, neurotic, about Scandinavian music, the surface melodic prettiness belying a fundamental starkness, goblin music; she switched it off. She gave in. No use trying to defer thinking about the David situation; no use trying to push it to the back of the drawer like an Income Tax demand.

He'd be somewhere along the motorway by now. Dear David. Poor David. Altogether too transparent for Emma, who needed clever concealment of essential stability for any relationship to be tenable. Poor Emma. Always risking everything on one throw, going out and seeking disaster. At whatever time she chose to lift the telephone receiver tonight, she'd learn of her father's death and, being Emma, she'd see it as some kind of judgment upon herself. Poor Geraldine. Never to be free of Emma. Eternal impingement. Poor everybody.

This afternoon, Emma's husband kissed me. If I'd been sixteen, or twenty-one— Apparently you reach an age when revenge loses its sweetness. I told him a lot of things, but I didn't tell him the one thing he has the most right to know and the one thing that would finally shatter those tinted spectacles through which he's viewed Emma for all these years. I never will tell him. Not because of loyalty, or ethics or any of that rubbish. Just because it's irrelevant. Because Emma is Emma and she can't alter her nature. Besides, every time I consider Emma, somehow it's like seeing myself reflected the wrong way round.

Leaning back against the cushions, she fancied she could still inhale some lingering trace of his presence and felt a spasm of physical longing. How much worse it would have been if her instinct of self-preservation hadn't asserted itself in time. But how long does one continue to preserve oneself? And is it any more praiseworthy than the alternative, Emma's suicide path?

Giving is what matters, he'd said. But for so long she'd regarded love as a premium on a policy of security and stability; she didn't think she was able to give any more unless she could be assured that what she gave would be increased threefold before it was returned to her. She'd crawled before Dennis, prepared to sell her soul for him, and in the end he'd despised her for it. Only two sorts of inhabitants in the emotional world, as far as she could see : the wounders and those who let themselves be wounded.

She'd realized early that she belonged to the latter category and therefore decided to retire to the rearguard in the field of action. Hadn't opted for the usual alternative either : the safe relationship constructed upon mutual affection. And there *had* been one or two men she could have married, with whom life could doubtless have been perfectly satis-factory, if passionless. Emma had once said that it was very easy to confuse friendship with love. Of course, she'd said, friendship was what most people wanted anyway, but if you didn't happen to be one of those people, the failure to distinguish could be disastrous. Emma had hoped her relationship with David would develop into something more, but had found that love behaved in a much more arbitrary fashion : 'It's nothing to do with liking. In fact, it's often the reverse. You might loathe him, his characteristics, all he represents, but you know that you must go ahead. It's positively atavistic—liking has nothing to do with it at all. I like David. I think you'd have to go a long way to find a truer person than David, but the man I loved—it didn't matter about those things. Perhaps it's just the bastard in me recognizing the bastard in someone else.'

Instant recognition. No law to say when your moment of instant recognition had to occur. It could even be, if you were lucky, after you'd grown to like each other. Surely that was the combination which made up your mind for you.

A headline from a paper she'd bought that afternoon caught her eye : 'Sterilized mother of seven pregnant again.' To have babies that looked like David, cook David's meals, fill hot-water-bottles when he had the 'flu— Ridiculous. That train of thought reminded her of being seventeen and seeing every attractive male in terms of how he'd look in a morning suit in front of the altar. Obviously the years change nothing except one's sophistic ability. At thirty-one she knew she was as incapable of loving with reservations as she'd been at seventeen. There was nothing to choose between herself and Emma, except that she recognized the necessity to conform to opinion, whereas Emma didn't think it worth the bother.

She opened her eyes. The clock face was beginning to look more like a clock face. He wouldn't be far from home now. Not long before he'd be driving up to that house which had always struck Geraldine as being as elegant and impersonal as a suite in a classy hotel. She'd visited it three times and each time had been unable to suppress sounds of disapproval when Emma carelessly put down hot dishes on polished surfaces or flicked cigarette ash without bothering to ascertain direction. Emma, standing in front of the dressing-table mirror, saying, 'For God's sake, ash is *good* for carpets. I read it only yesterday in a Woman's What-not.'

'I don't think it's so good for white lace bedspreads.'

And Emma spat on her forefinger and attempted to erase the mark, without success. 'There's a woman who lives in this road—kids have grown up and left, husband comes home only when there's nowhere else to go—who has been known to Hoover the carpet at two a.m. and who redecorates approximately every three weeks. Christ Gerry, there are so many more *important* things than houses and the objects you put inside them. I can do without those kind of compulsions, thank you very much.'

Only because you have other, stronger, but equally fruitless compulsions, Geraldine had thought.

But, even for Emma, flattery had ceased to be enough and so she'd apparently involved herself in a full-blooded *affaire* : stolen hours, snatched drinks, every meeting accompanied by an exquisite tension, the world of the minor key; Emma acting out the plaintive fatalism of a French ballad, reading romantic nuances into situations that were the very antithesis of romance.

And I will never allow myself to take part in that sort of self-deception. Her own vehemence surprised her. Meeting David for an afternoon, a night, always aware at the moment of meeting of the inevitable moment of parting. Living in a box, waiting for him to lift the lid for a brief, glorious interval, knowing that she had to be replaced and the lid shut down again. All right, she wanted David. But she hadn't been through the torments of unrequited love quite in vain. Nothing could gauge the misery of loving someone who was not able to return love to that same degree. Illicit love was fine where it belonged—in the French ballads; *she* knew she was intelligent enough and independent enough to have a happy love affair and that accepting anything less would be an insult to her self-respect.

She thawed two lamb chops from the fridge, fed the dog and began to peel potatoes. Just as if nothing had happened. But at least one irrevocable thing had happened; Robert Sainter might almost have timed his death as a final touch of dramatic irony.

She remembered her own father's death, six years ago. He was a withdrawn man, ill at ease with children; in that house of constant washing and polishing and bed-making, an insubstantial figure who left it at eight and returned to it at seven, who was quite overshadowed by his wife's vitality and seemingly content to be so. Geraldine had been upset when he died, but rather more by the idea that she was fatherless than because an irreplaceable individual had been removed from her life. It would not be the same for Emma. There'd been more facets in *that* relationship than met the eye; she'd been his pretty, pampered, only child, his substitute wife perhaps, later the partner who was aware of and condoned his deceptions. She remembered that dinner, long, long ago, the grace and the courtesy of it and, for Emma, no doubt, the glamour of conspiracy. Perhaps all that old-hat stuff about parental standards meant something after all. Perhaps breaking down the conventional barriers like that had been a dreadful mistake.

And if Robert Sainter hadn't died yesterday she would probably not have found herself in this situation. Emma would have returned, interlude undetected, marriage to jog along as before. What blame we can lay at the door of coincidence. But then coincidence is only the starting point. It's up to ourselves whether we accept or reject the forces of circumstance and the way they're pointing.

Above the sink, her reflection in the window pane startled her. She began to understand Emma and her mirror obsession. Gazing not only to see a reflection, but that she might come to understand herself by that reflection, that she might see *what* it was the mirror showed. Unaware that that was a knowledge that could only be imparted from without, through other people.

He'd write, he'd said. He would too. And he was a man she could love. And make him love her too. For once in her life, she held a winning hand. Whether she put it to use, or she didn't, the fact she held it remained.

That night in the hotel Majestic, two revelling drunks took exception to the barman's refusal to serve them and removed their jackets. The police were summoned and three straight-faced constables tried a short, vain period of reasoning, then dragged the offenders, cursing and struggling, out through the doors of the lounge bar, breaking a pane of glass in the fray. An old lady who'd been enjoying a quiet glass of Guinness became over-excited and fainted and was, in the chaos, inadvertently revived with, not the ordinary stuff that was kept for such emergencies, but Courvoisier.

The occupants of room 204, double with bath, were never to know of the night's alarms; the police siren, wailing along the main road, woke even the deaf lady in 220, but was unheard by Patrick and Emma, engaged in their own interlocking strife.

Dying so many times in that night with her hands on his back, only to be roused to die again. She, who had previously held romantic love as her ideal, found that romance had nothing at all to do with it. This was sensuality, sharp and sweet, and it left her with a desperate thirst that could only be assuaged by him, and him again. Away from him, lying awake in the darkness, she would be seized by physical memory and with it fear, in case it should continue to plague her after their affair was over. Self-taught from literature, she'd believed that you had to love a man emotionally before you could love him physically. She'd been quite unprepared to discover that the reverse could be true.

Her right arm, beneath his shoulders, was going into cramp and if there's one thing to banish passion, it's cramp. She extricated it gently, but he grunted and woke.

'You forgot to remind me,' she said, pushing tangled hair out of his half-open eyes, thinking that men were like little boys when they woke, calling forth maternal instincts you never knew you possessed.

'Remind you about what?'

'My telephone call.'

He turned over to her, a heaving of muscle and bed-clothes. 'Do it now. I'll go into the loo and plug my ears.'

'At eleven-thirty? He'd wonder what deathly quiet place I was inhabiting at eleven-thirty. Never mind. I didn't make it a definite arrangement. He'll merely think stupid, absent-minded Emma. And anyway, if you plug up your ears, you won't hear the sirens' music.'

'Who needs sirens' music?' Limbs heavy, the desire for sleep fighting with the desire for love, he drew his hand across the contours of her body. 'I want you so much. I feel like Thor, or whoever it was, who had to drain a drinking horn whose end was placed in the sea. All because I have to cram a month into three nights.'

Moonlight and snowglare filtering through the woven curtains, she could see the outline of his face but needed her fingers to trace its terrain. The skin beneath his eyes was touchingly tender and prone to wrinkle. 'What does she think when you go home yawning and with shadows under your eyes?'

'I say "Oh, those endless dinners and drinks and those awful hotel beds." Not that she really looks at me any more anyway.'

'Don't you ever have the desire to boast? To say that you spent last night in the arms of someone else, making delicious love till daybreak? Perhaps it isn't the desire to boast at all, perhaps it's the need to share such a tremendous experience.'

'I know what you mean. It's the downfall of many an affair. You just can't resist using the private phrase in public. You need to make it known that part-ownership of the other person exists.'

'Then it's lucky that Beryl and I don't move in the same circles. After a couple of drinks I should be bound to be indiscreet.'

A quick, involuntary shudder of fear that he tried to stifle. There were ways and ways of finding out. Who could say which, if any, was the least painful? And, unlike Emma, he had a child to consider, a child in whom he could already discern his own charms and weaknesses. He didn't want to lose the child, his trophy, possibly the only worthwhile thing he'd ever been responsible for. Emma would not be able to understand that. There was something about seeing the child, thin and brown in khaki shorts, standing with furious concentration at the wicket of the back garden fence on an August afternoon, that cancelled out the sterility of the marriage.

He dozed and dreamed about the child and woke to touch emptiness. Momentary panic before he threw off the last shred of the dream and saw the red glow of a cigarette end by the window.

She moved back to the bed and, kneeling, cradled his head against soft flesh and blue frills. 'You were talking.'

'What did I say?' Alarmed at the possibility of subconscious disloyalty.

'Mumble, mumble, labels, mumble, mumble.'

'Labels?'

'Perhaps you're anticipating a long voyage.'

'Can't you sleep?'

She felt for the ashtray, found it and stubbed out her cigarette. 'Never can. Your proximity makes sleep difficult to come by. Who needs sleep anyway? I can sleep for a week after tonight if I want to.'

The matter-of-fact bleakness of her tone made him feel boorish. The least he could do was to keep awake, keep vigil with her on this, their last night. He switched on the bedside lamp and touched her forehead with a contrite kiss.

'Poor Patrick. It's easier for me, isn't it? I'm only a woman who follows along in the wake of her man. I have little to lose, or, at least, less than you. It's you who has to make decisions and face consequences and things.'

She sat cross-legged beside him, the folds and frills of her dressing-gown falling away from her like petals from a stamen. It was one of those moments that might not occur again, when she could regard the situation tenderly, realistically and without rancour. She'd talked of tunes and fragrances as souvenirs; it was instants like these he would wish to preserve in formalin, labelled as 'that moment when I and a woman called Emma could look at each other in complete truth and yet continue to love.'

'The way things are,' she continued, 'nobody gets hurt. Our lives and possibly their lives are enriched because of it. But the moment we attempt to disturb the status quo, everything will be thrown into desperate confusion, because we'll be basing our love on two other people's misery. It isn't the whole horrific paraphernalia of divorce—private detectives in league with chambermaids and obliging, respectable ladies in Bayswater hotels and all the sordidness of dividing incomes—that's the deterrent, it's the knowledge that you can't live with remorse.'

She paused for breath. 'That's why, now, while I have the courage, it's better to ask you whether or not we had better draw a neat little line underneath it while it's still good.' She fumbled for another cigarette, fingers entangled in silver paper and cellophane. He took the packet from her, lit one and placed it in her mouth.

'I dread the rot setting in, of one day receiving a letter or a phone call to say it's over, because that I don't think I could bear. Better, if we must, to write finis when we're face to face.'

He held the cigarette between her lips while she drew on it and tried to ease her back into his arms, but she resisted. 'Do you think I could say all this with you holding me?'

'But why now Emma? What's suddenly forced the issue?'

'I don't know. Whim. A feeling of angst when I was lying awake and you were asleep, away from me, muttering about labels. All the morbid thoughts that assail me when we're apart came rushing to the fore. At the beginning, it

was all so light-hearted and gay. I didn't give a damn about
her. My view was that it's jungle warfare and if she can't
take the trouble to learn the tactics, I have no sympathy for
her. But tonight, beside you, unaccountably, I began to
think of my father and how my mother must have felt all
these years, how—degraded she must have felt. We can
play-act between ourselves, but other people's suffering
isn't play-acting, it's real.'

He lay flat on his back and very still. He knew what he
might say during the next few minutes could influence his
immediate future. 'I should have thought that you'd realized the play-acting quality evaporated pretty quickly.
About five years ago, there was another girl, a nice, ordinary
girl without a predisposition towards married men, but I
pursued her until she'd fallen in love with me, then I didn't
want her any more. She got over it of course, that's one of
the advantages of base humanity, we get over things, but I
still believe that she carries an unnecessary scar. You were
an adventure for me too at first. But it's ceased to be like
that. And I am not letting you go away from me tomorrow
morning thinking that we meant nothing more than a diversion for each other.'

But, as with all his statements, there was a sensible rider
tacked on to the end : 'No promises, Emma. I'm not giving
you any promises. Nor do I want any from you. Perhaps
we'll be together, perhaps we'll try being apart and see if
we can keep our sanity. I just don't know. Time's the
criminal. If I could have met you before I married—'

'Before you married, I was sitting at a wooden desk con-
jugating Latin verbs. And not realizing that I'd have to
wait so long for the man who was marked out for me.'

'And now you find it's not at all the way you thought it
would be.'

'It's just the way I thought it would be. During one's

adolescence no romance is complete without an element of tragedy. It's funny, isn't it, how only yesterday, years ago, I was saying that I couldn't suppress my happiness when I'm with you?'

'It's the only thing that makes the rest of it worthwhile,' he said firmly, opening the covers to her.

His body was at once comfortingly familiar and excitingly strange. Not a particularly beautiful man; David was more conventionally handsome, not until he held her like this and then every part of him filled her with an ecstasy of delight: the cruciform blaze of curling hair on his chest, the long thighs where the hair grew differently, straight and soft, the scar which ran vertically through one eyebrow where no hair grew, and the eyes themselves, disturbingly opaque, lover's eyes—unique.

And he, with all his resources, pledged his sincerity in this last token. Tomorrow morning would be hurried: Continental breakfast, bites of toast and the buzz of an electric razor, searching twice and rapidly after the cases were packed, in case they'd left anything that might be posted on to an address that didn't exist, then a jumpy station farewell, for his other life claimed him again tomorrow. Tomorrow they'd be stunned with lack of sleep and the amputation of parting. Tonight was the real goodbye. At least he could make it a goodbye she'd remember.

Friday

Emma picked up a British Railways tea-tray, walked along a passage bounded by steel rails, fancied none of British Railways atrocities behind glass so felt foolish with a solitary cup of coffee isolated among acres of brown plastic.

One more station buffet, a seat where she could see the hands of the clock, apparently petrified, an assortment of social dregs around and about her. Only two hours ago there'd been another station buffet, it could have been the same one, and two coffees and it had been as awful as she'd anticipated. In the first place, he'd had to drive round in circles for fifteen minutes before he found a parking space. And then he'd been told not to stay too long by a jaundiced railway employee. So, for ten minutes, they'd forced conversation, fiddling with blue plastic tea-spoons, looking anywhere but at each other. As always, she believed that she would never see him again, that, away from her, all the words and smiles and touches would be forgotten. Then a brushing of lips against cheek by the bookstall, with a dozen people looking on; funny how uninhibited one could be when *meeting* somebody at a railway station, yet when it came to farewells, it seemed as though the eyes of the world were watching. 'I'll phone you.' And, briefcase in his hand, he turned a corner and was gone. Left with a million things unsaid, she'd walked the length of the train to avoid getting into a compartment full of those who'd been observing them.

And now here she was, waiting for the connection that would disgorge her into the maelstrom of Euston. Not unbearable yet though. She was still buoyed up with almost tangible recollections. Desolation would arrive with Watford or, if she was lucky, Harrow, when all the seasoned commuters were buttoning up their overcoats and all the strangers were thinking surely *this* can't be London, but too shy of showing themselves up as raw provincials to ask. That's when it would strike, increasing as she ran down the steps of the Underground, infected with the general scramble, though there was no need for her to rush, magnifying as she changed lines from black to blue and finally engulfing her as she put the key into the lock of her smart French navy front door.

There were no empty compartments on the train; she was forced to occupy a seat uncomfortably opposite somebody else. She hoped somebody else, of whom only a hairy wrist, a cuff and one of a flamboyant pair of cuff-links were visible behind his paper, was not feeling gregarious. He wasn't. When she lit a cigarette, a fierce pair of eyebrows appeared over the top of the paper and an immaculate, nicotine-free forefinger indicated the no-smoking sign. Chastened, she pulled down her case from the rack and moved backwards into the general crowded fug.

This time the only available seat was that opposite what could only be a returning honeymoon couple. Emma was filled with distaste by their defencelessness; everything about them proclaimed that they hadn't yet grasped the full implications of being married : bright, oversized and ostentatious ring (her hands were red and blue with cold but gloves would have been unthinkable), incongruous white coat, straight out of the trousseau department, ornamented with a bunch of artificial cherries, he, with his rough, square hands and shiny blue suit. For a moment, Emma was touched that they could look so awful and love each other in spite of it. Of course, upon reflection, there was no in spite of it at all, they just didn't realize they looked awful. But they were in love and they were together, holding hands and not exchanging a word as the train's rhythm changed from Birmingham, to Euston, Euston, and for that reason alone she hated them.

She closed her eyes, vainly trying to conjure up an image of him, any image: Patrick grave, Patrick smiling, Patrick trying to fasten his cuff-links, a supreme example of more haste, less speed. Like all the other times, she found it impossible. She could recall in clearest outline David's face, the daily help's face, the face of the woman in the kiosk where she bought her cigarettes, any face but his face. She didn't even have a photograph, there was nowhere to keep a photograph. His occasional letters had to be mingled among other, unimportant ones and locked in the bureau—even then she was certain that some day she'd leave the key lying about and David, though not prone to baseness of that sort, was human after all. She wondered if Patrick was plagued by the inadequacy of memory, driving on to his real life, busily adapting his business persona. Unlikely.

A waiter came along the aisle, proffering coffee. Sometimes she thought that the one abiding impression of their association would be the cups of coffee. Blue serge and ripe cherries availed themselves of the service: digestive biscuits, ham sandwiches—she ate one to his three, silently, in a state of grace that can dispense with words. So, in a few years, they'd be another Emma and David, silent because they had nothing to say to one another, but that didn't ease the pain of having to observe their present glory. Emma opened her magazine and discovered that everyone would be wearing yellow next season. It would be their first summer together, if they were still together. Her imagination encircled scenes of white beaches and sparkling seas and fields full of buttercups, backdrops for the two of them, she golden, he darker, exposing lithe limbs to a bronze disc that would blaze day after shimmering day, while they swam and slept and made love in a sheltered bay. There was no hesitation or boredom on the shingles of her imaginary summer coastlines.

Next time they met, she vowed she'd be less prickly—his rejection of her ancient woes was, after all, a natural masculine reaction—for, despite her attempt the previous night at false heroics, the idea of no next time was unbearable. It wasn't that she couldn't envisage life without him—she could, with dismal ease, it stretched ahead of her, a grey vista of dullness. The state of being in love caused everything previously boring and insignificant to pulse with a verdant life, clearing your gaze to see the blueness of hyacinths or the surprising aesthetic satisfaction of a slum skyline. Losing him would mean losing all that. She just *couldn't* go back to how it was before.

The landscape became less snowbound as they neared London. It almost made her laugh to think that only a river separated their homes, yet it was necessary for them to travel miles to be together. In her youth, discussing the time when they'd be free, fast women carrying on gay, wistful *affaires* with soigné men, they'd always plumped for London as having the best possibilities for anonymity. It had turned out to be untrue. Occasionally they chanced a furtive lunchtime drink in a bar, with him behaving towards her as if she was a business acquaintance in case he saw anyone he knew. Even dinner at an inn on the edge of the Cotswolds had found them seated at the next table to one of his neighbours. She, on the other hand, more totally committed, took risks with less qualms. Once, she'd taken a train, the Underground and a bus, just to weigh up the opposition in Beryl's boutique, but had, apparently, chosen the wrong day, because the two identically-clad females she saw as she pretended to flick through rows of dresses couldn't have been more than nineteen. It was a ridiculously juvenile impulse she'd regretted and hadn't succumbed to again.

In the jolting lavatory someone had written 'Molly loves Patrick.' An Irish double-act. She wondered if Molly's Patrick had been free to love Molly. Unlikely. If everything's hunky-dory you don't have to write it on walls. She peered, with difficulty, into the mirror. Her skin felt tight and warm, the effect of no sleep, and her lips sore with kissing. But, thankfully, the closest of scrutineers would have been hard put to it to discern the fact. Perhaps the thankfully was a lie. Didn't she sometimes, out of temper, burn to taunt David with reference to a lover? Wouldn't it, in a certain way, be a relief to cross the Rubicon?

Back in the compartment, she had to admit that no, it would not be a relief. She might be left stranded and how could she possibly cope then? There'd be nobody to *see* to things; she'd never been any use at seeing to things. Besides there had to be someone in whose company you could drop your façades, be yourself, your dull, inadequate, selfish self, someone who knew better than to expect too much from you.

Different of course if Patrick wanted to marry her. Different altogether. Other people were divorced. Always other people though. Her father had never attempted that final break. Cowardice or compassion? She thought the latter. It was almost a year since she'd been home. She could still think of that new, brick bungalow with its neurotically symmetrical pathways and privet hedges as home. Not that she didn't want to go. It was just that during these past months her time had become a blank diary waiting for

Patrick's entries and it would have been aggravating to have made some definite arrangement, only to find that it coincided with his free time. But perhaps the day had now come to seek the second opinion she'd been too frightened to seek years ago. If anyone could tell her the advantages and disadvantages of drastic action, it was her father. And now she thought she'd grown sufficiently far away from him to be able to ask. She'd ask him why, all those years ago, he hadn't gone to Flora. Was it because of her mother, or because of herself? Or was it because the idea of loss of face, the inevitable indignity, was repellent to him? She'd ask him if anything didn't justify the chasing away of boredom. He should be an authority on that at least. He'd spent a lifetime battling against it. She'd go next weekend and smile the smile that clinched their complicity. She'd be Emma the child again, not to be scolded because children can't be held responsible for their actions. Anyway, he'd always be there, whatever happened.

Meanwhile she'd be nicer to David. In a way, it was good to be going home to David. Passion is so exhausting. Nobody would want to live on that level *all* the time.

Watford. And not feeling nearly as desolate as she'd imagined. She leaned back in her seat, stretching tired limbs. Things not to forget : write a thank-you letter to Gerry. Good old Geraldine. So little loyalty about these days. Try to do all those boring wifely things with a bit more zest in the future. Concentrate on the ordinary and then the other reality, when next it occurs, will seem like a gift.

Seven miles to Euston. She looked across at blue serge who gallantly responded and lifted down her case. Two o'clock. David should be back from lunch by now. She might even ring him from the station to say she was home.